P9-BZJ-579

The Stolen Gold Affair

Carpenter and Quincannon Mysteries

BY MARCIA MULLER AND BILL PRONZINI

The Bughouse Affair

The Spook Lights Affair

The Body Snatchers Affair

The Plague of Thieves Affair

The Dangerous Ladies Affair

BY BILL PRONZINI

The Bags of Tricks Affair

The Flimflam Affair

The Stolen Gold Affair

The Stolen Gold Affair

A CARPENTER AND QUINCANNON MYSTERY

BILL PRONZINI

A TOM DOHERTY ASSOCIATES BOOK

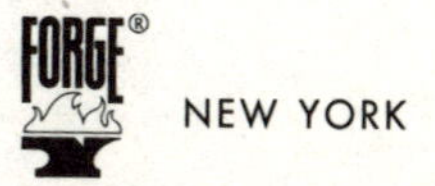

NEW YORK

This is a work of fiction. All of the characters, organizations, and events portrayed in this novel are either products of the author's imagination or are used fictitiously.

THE STOLEN GOLD AFFAIR

A Forge Book
Published by Tom Doherty Associates
120 Broadway
New York, NY 10271

www.tor-forge.com

Forge® is a registered trademark of Macmillan Publishing Group, LLC.

The Library of Congress Cataloging-in-Publication Data is available upon request.

ISBN 978-1-250-21648-9 (hardcover)
ISBN 978-1-250-21649-6 (ebook)

Our books may be purchased in bulk for promotional, educational, or business use. Please contact your local bookseller or the Macmillan Corporate and Premium Sales Department at 1-800-221-7945, extension 5442, or by email at MacmillanSpecialMarkets@macmillan.com.

First Edition: April 2020

Printed in the United States of America

0 9 8 7 6 5 4 3 2 1

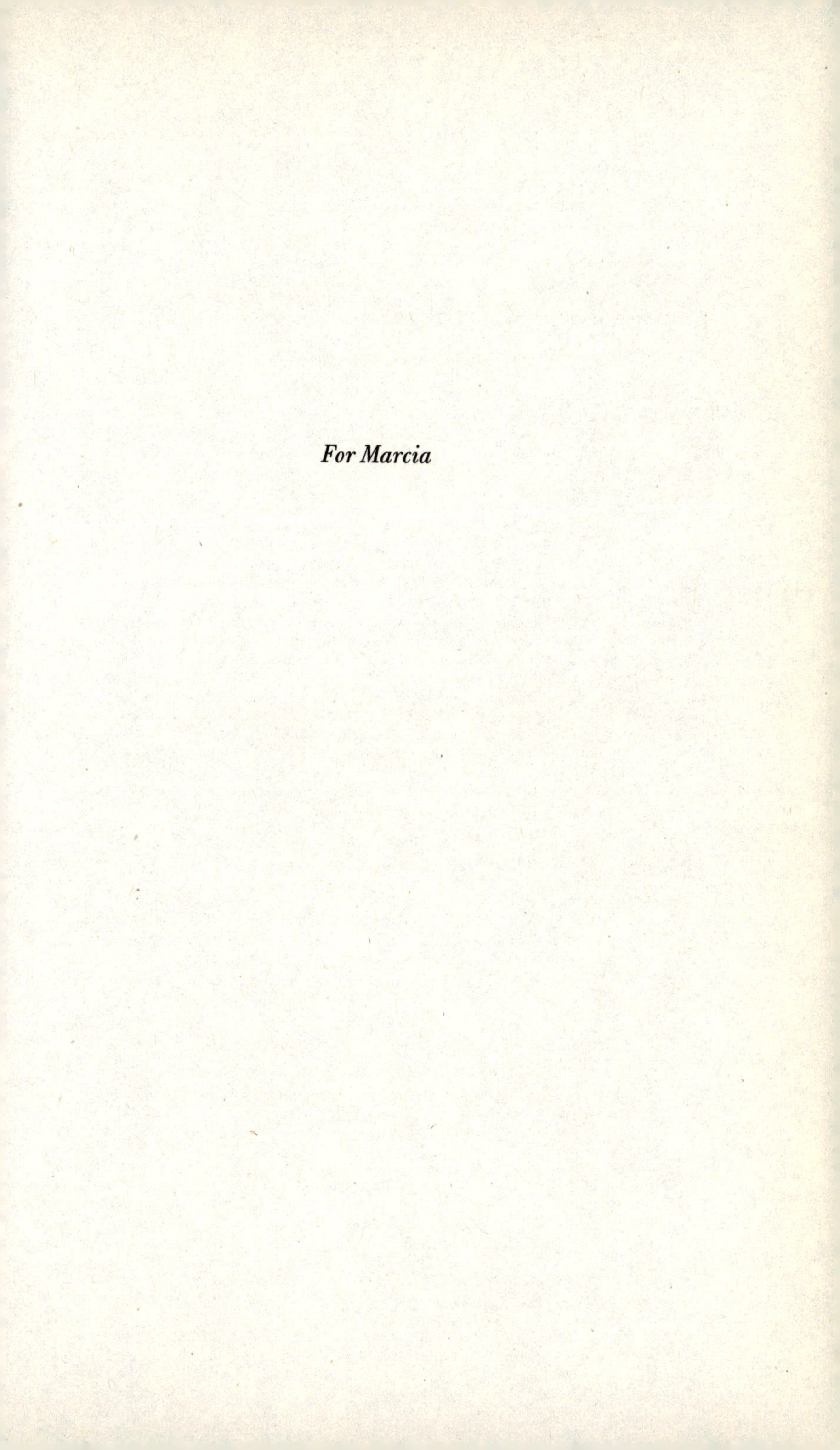

For Marcia

The Stolen Gold Affair

1

QUINCANNON

The Olympic Club, San Francisco's venerable men's athletic and social club, was housed in a new four-story brick and masonry pile on Post and Mason streets, more or less cheek by jowl with the home of the city's even more exclusive all-male fraternal organization, the Bohemian Club. The present clubhouse had opened in 1893 to no small amount of fanfare; the Olympic itself had been in existence for nearly forty years, the brainchild of two German brothers and fitness enthusiasts. Such prominent San Franciscans as Charles Crocker and Leland Stanford were among the Olympic's members, as was Gentleman Jim Corbett, winner of the 1892 world heavyweight prizefighting title. Samuel Clemens, better known under his pen name Mark Twain, had been a frequent visitor during his newspapering days.

Quincannon was neither a member of the club nor a regular guest. Its various attractions—gymnastic equipment, boxing facilities, steam rooms, a large natatorium filled with salt water from a pipeline that extended all the way downtown from Ocean Beach—held no appeal for him. Neither did the sporting events such as rugby and tennis that the Olympic sponsored. Athletics were all well and good, but he kept himself in excellent physical shape by his own devices, often enough as a consequence of the cases he was called upon to investigate. And when it came to social interaction, he preferred the fellowship of friends and valued business acquaintances to that of either the cloistered rich or the sporting young.

He passed through the club's arched Post Street entrance at five minutes shy of noon on a blustery late October day. As with his only other visit three years previous, he was there on a business matter, though in this instance he had been invited by one of the members. The invitation had come by messenger, and though the message hadn't specified the reason for the requested meeting, he had wasted no time in sending an affirmative reply. The identity of the sender was a more than sufficient lure: Everett Hoxley was among the city's wealthiest men, the head of a large corporation that owned several gold and silver mines in northern California and Nevada.

Quincannon presented his name and card at the reception desk in the high-ceilinged lobby and was immediately conducted by a young attendant to a private alcove in the bar/restaurant. Two men were seated at the table there; neither of them rose or offered to shake hands when the attendant announced, "Mr. John Quincannon." He was not offended. Gentlemen of means sometimes failed to observe the niceties with individuals they considered beneath their station, and he didn't mind being patronized as long as there was a chance he would be amply rewarded.

The older of the two gave him a long appraising look. He seemed to approve of what he saw; he nodded once, vigorously, after which he looked up at a large wall clock and said, "Precisely noon. Very good, I like a man who keeps his appointments on time. I am Everett Hoxley."

"At your service, sir."

"I hope you shall be," Hoxley said, and nodded again. He had lived fifty years, if the newspaper articles about him were accurate, but he might have passed for a gent on the near side of forty. Lean and trimly fit, smooth-shaven cheeks a healthy hue, gray-green eyes clear and bright, authoritative demeanor showing the same vigor as his nods. He obviously made regular use of the club's facilities. He wore an expensive light gray business suit, but there was no question that he would strike an equally impressive figure in athletic garb. "Be seated, Mr. Quincannon."

The table was set for luncheon, but there was nothing edible on it, nor any bills of fare. This told Quincannon that his invitation did not include sharing a meal with Mr. Hoxley and his companion unless he agreed to whatever proposition the mining entrepreneur had summoned him to discuss.

When he occupied the table's only vacant chair, Hoxley introduced the other man as James O'Hearn. Just who O'Hearn was he didn't say, but to Quincannon's practiced eye the man bore the stamp of a hardrock miner out of his element. He was as unlike Hoxley as it was possible to be. Matted brown hair thicker and more coarse than Quincannon's whiskers covered his face, likewise his wrists, the backs of his fingers, and no doubt the rest of him except for the crown of his head, which was as barren as a desert knob. The overall image he presented was that of a scalped grizzly bear stuffed into an ill-fitting broadcloth suit. It was plain that even in these genteel surroundings he would have been more comfortable in miner's garb. No refined athlete, O'Hearn. Whip-hand mine boss and barroom brawler was more like it.

A white-jacketed waiter approached and hovered. Hoxley asked, "Would you care for a libation, Mr. Quincannon?"

"Only if warm clam juice is available."

It wasn't. Hoxley waved the waiter away without ordering anything for himself and O'Hearn, to the latter's apparent displeasure. Then he said to Quincannon, "You are not a drinking man?"

"No, sir."

Another approving nod. "Neither am I. Alcohol, in my view, is a detriment to good health and clear judgment."

From the way O'Hearn's crop of whiskers twitched, he didn't agree. The whiskers had also twitched at Quincannon's stated preference for warm clam juice, a drink he obviously considered unsavory if not unmanly.

"I do not believe in wasting time or breath," Hoxley said, "so I will get right to the point. You have been recommended as a highly competent investigator willing to undertake difficult assignments. True?"

"True enough. Though if I may say so, 'highly competent' doesn't quite describe my abilities."

"No? How would you describe them?"

"As unparalleled. There is no better detective in the Western states."

O'Hearn grunted and spoke for the first time in a growly voice that matched his bearlike appearance. "Think a lot of yourself, don't you?"

"With just cause. My accomplishments speak for themselves."

"I like a man who speaks plainly and without false modesty," Hoxley said with yet another head bob. "You have no fear of undertaking a potentially hazardous investigation?"

The question caused an involuntary response: Quincannon lifted a hand to almost but not quite finger his mutilated left ear. A counterfeiter's bullet had torn off the earlobe less than two months ago. He was no longer quite so self-conscious about the disfigurement, thanks mostly to Sabina, but he had yet to completely lose the notion that people were wont to stare at the ear, or to end his habit of probing at it.

"None," he said, "if it isn't of a foolhardy nature." And if the fee is large enough, he thought but didn't add.

"What do you know about gold mining? Specifically, the physical operation of a large mine."

"A fair amount."

"In principle or from personal experience?"

"Both. I once worked as a laborer in such a mine."

"Here in California?"

"No. Back East." He saw no reason to explain that it had been a brief and none too satisfactory summer job in his youth.

O'Hearn said, "Gold mining's different out here."

"No doubt. But the basic labor practices are the same."

"Where'd you work, topside or down below?"

"Both."

"At what levels below?"

"Seven hundred and eight hundred feet."

"Not so deep. Doing what?"

"Member of the timber crew."

Hoxley said, "Would you be willing and able to undertake such work now?"

"You mean adopt the guise of a hardrock miner?"

"It would be necessary, yes. Do you feel you could pose as one well enough to avoid detection?"

Undercover work. Quincannon had no objection to that; he had done a fair and varied amount of it over the years, most recently as a mixologist in a Grass Valley saloon and gaming parlor. "I have no doubt that I could," he said. "For what purpose?"

"To identify the individuals responsible for an insidious high-grading operation in a mine owned by Hoxley and Associates, and to put a satisfactory end to their activities. You know what high-grading is, of course."

Quincannon acknowledged that he knew high-grading was the surreptitious theft of ore or dust from inside a gold mine by one or more members of its mining crews. He said then, "Large amounts of gold are being stolen, I assume?"

"Very large amounts, by our reckoning. We don't know how much, of course, but the production of high-quality ore in this mine has dropped noticeably in the past few months."

"An organized gang of thieves, then."

"Has to be," O'Hearn said. "As many as half a dozen men working on each of three shifts."

"Have you any idea who they are?"

"No. There have been rumors of the high-grading, but special company men posted in the crews failed to come up with any definite information. If anyone knows or suspects who the thieves are, they're keeping it to themselves."

"Special company men" was a euphemism for informant miners paid extra to keep an eye on their fellows and to report any slacking or other rule breaks. It was no surprise that the ones posted by O'Hearn had failed to learn anything. Such spies were often known or suspected by their fellows, and untrained in the art of detection in any case; the high-graders would be careful to neither act nor converse in the presence of anyone other than one of their own.

"We do have our eye on one man," O'Hearn went on, "but he isn't directly connected with the mine."

"A local resident?"

"No. Newcomer and hanger-on."

"Who is he? What makes you suspicious of him?"

O'Hearn glanced at his employer, who gave a small headshake. "We're not ready to discuss that just yet," he said to Quincannon.

"How do you suppose the gold is being taken out of the mine?"

"Damned cleverly, however it's being done. All we know for certain is that it's not in any of the usual ways."

Of which there were many, Quincannon knew. The most common was for mine workers to conceal chunks of gold-bearing ore in lunch pails, double or false-crowned hats, inside long socks or cloth tubes hung inside trouser legs, in pockets sewn into canvas corset covers worn beneath the shirt. As much as five pounds of high-grade ore could be carried out in those ways. But the amount of pure gold to be obtained by smuggling in such fashion was relatively small, and the functionaries whose job it was to inspect miners and their clothing at the end of each shift would have soon caught thieves using any of those ploys. The methods used by an organized group pilfering large amounts had to be much more sophisticated.

O'Hearn added in his bear's growl, "If my men and I haven't been able to get to the bottom of it, I don't see how an outsider can. No matter how smart a detective he thinks he is."

"*Knows* he is," Quincannon corrected. "You're the superintendent of this mine, Mr. O'Hearn?"

"That's right."

"Located in California, is it?"

O'Hearn glanced at Hoxley again before answering in the affirmative.

"The location?"

Hoxley said, "We will divulge that and provide you with all other pertinent data if you consent to undertake the commission. Do you consent?"

Quincannon would have liked to buy more time before responding by packing and lighting his Dublin briar, but for all he knew the Olympic Club frowned on the use of tobacco in its public rooms. Even if they didn't, Hoxley surely would. He started to finger his ear again, caught himself, and fluffed his beard instead.

At length he said, "It promises to be a task that can't be done quickly or easily."

"That it does," Hoxley agreed. "I am prepared to financially underwrite your investigation for one month, longer if absolutely necessary. Your standard per diem fee plus all travel and other expenses. And a bonus if you succeed in exposing the responsible individuals and their methods. I am a generous man when circumstances warrant it, as Mr. O'Hearn can attest. That is how vitally important this matter is to Hoxley and Associates."

Now Quincannon was in an even deeper quandary. As many as four weeks at what would be the highest per diem fees charged by Carpenter and Quincannon, Professional Detective Services. All expenses paid. Generous bonus. And the sort of challenge he thrived on. There was only one problem. And it wasn't a small one.

Hoxley misinterpreted his silence. "Do you have some other pressing business that might prevent you from accepting?"

Yes, as a matter of fact, he did. But he couldn't very well say, "My partner, Sabina Carpenter, and I are planning to be married soon." It would make him sound like a dolt. The date had been set for the last Saturday of the month, a little less than three weeks from now. Then again, preparations had only just begun; it was not too late to table them temporarily. Sabina would understand, and agree to a brief postponement. Wouldn't she?

"Well, Mr. Quincannon?"

He hedged a bit longer by saying, "You would want me to begin immediately, I trust?"

"Tomorrow at the latest."

"Will you wait until later today for my decision?" After he had had a chance to speak with Sabina, he was thinking.

Hoxley's headshake was as vigorous as his nods. "I must have it now. Time is of the essence. Mr. O'Hearn will be departing this afternoon to return to his duties at the mine. If you decline, I will be forced to seek another suitable candidate, no small task on short notice as I am sure you realize."

And he would not be pleased about having to do so, perhaps to the point of taking the good name of John Frederick Quincannon in vain to peers who might also one day be in the need of investigative services. That was evident in Hoxley's expression and tone.

Accept the lucrative assignment or turn it down? Plainly he was the man Hoxley preferred, the best man for such daunting undercover work. And as always his blood simmered at the prospect of a new and adventurous test of his skills. He chafed at the thought of postponing the wedding, of disappointing Sabina, of spending as many as four weeks away from her, yet it might not come to that; he might well complete the assignment quickly enough to keep the delay to a minimum. After all, confound it, business was business. They were not in the detective game for their health . . .

He said, "My answer, Mr. Hoxley, is yes."

And hoped he wouldn't regret it.

2

SABINA

Sabina Carpenter Quincannon.

Seated at her desk in the agency's Market Street office, she wrote the name in flowing script on a scrap of notepaper, not for the first time, then blotted the ink and once more examined the signature. It was long, and certainly a mouthful when spoken, but it read well and it had a nice, euphonious ring to it. How would it look on one of her business cards? She extracted one from the supply in her desk and carefully printed the new name above her present one. The result made her smile. It would look just fine on the fresh set of embossed cards she would order before the wedding.

She started to write the name another time, abruptly changed her mind, and put the pen back in its onyx holder. This was silly behavior, really. Schoolgirl stuff. She hadn't even indulged in it when she fell in love with Stephen at twenty-two and accepted his marriage proposal. Now she was past thirty, a widow and ardent suffragist, an emancipated woman functioning successfully in a virtually all-male profession. And it wasn't as if her relationship with John was brand new; she'd known and worked closely with him for seven years. It had taken a long time for her feelings for him, and his for her, to build to the kind of intimacy that had led him, a lifelong bachelor, to ask for her hand and for her to give her consent.

Before John, Stephen had been the only man in her life, the only man with whom she had shared a bed. After he had been wrenched from her by an outlaw's bullet in a skirmish outside Denver, she'd believed no one could ever take his place and she would never marry again, that she would remain celibate for the rest of her days. And so she had until the night a few short weeks ago when John clumsily but touchingly proposed to her.

She'd been brazen that night, so consumed by love and desire that she had amazed herself as well as John by quite literally seducing him. And she hadn't felt a bit guilty afterward. It was not in any way a betrayal of Stephen's memory, because it was not merely the scratching of a suppressed biological itch. It was a true act of love—that first time, and the three times . . . no, four . . . they had shared his bed since. After seven long years of self-endorsed celibacy, she had almost forgotten how pleasurable such intimacy could be.

Stephen had been a wonderful lover: gentle, considerate, always seeking to pleasure her as well as himself. So was John. Not that she would ever compare them, but she couldn't help thinking that John was . . . well, more experienced in the art of lovemaking. From years of long practice with numerous conquests, no doubt, not that his profligate past bothered or concerned her. The thought of their most recent coupling brought warmth out of the high collar of her lace-trimmed shirtwaist. Shameless woman. No. Just a woman in love for the second and final time.

She hadn't told or even hinted to her closest confidantes, Amity Wellman and Callie French, about the premarital consummations, though if she had she suspected that they would not have been disapproving. Callie, in fact, would probably have congratulated her for finally shedding her inhibitions. Her middle-aged cousin's plump, matronly demeanor concealed a permissive attitude and an occasionally ribald sense of humor (she had once intimated that she'd been something of a bawd in her youth). She was also an inveterate matchmaker; she'd actually cheered when Sabina told her of John's proposal and her acceptance.

Predictably, Callie had insisted on hosting the wedding at the Frenches' Van Ness Avenue mansion. Sabina, after consulting with John, had agreed on the firm condition that invitations were to be issued to just a select few of their friends and business acquaintances. If she'd given Callie carte blanche, the occasion would have evolved into an extravaganza, complete with an orchestra to play the Wedding March and a guest list that included members of the socially elite she barely knew. Even what Callie referred to as "small, intimate dinner parties" invariably turned into showcase affairs. It had been at one of those, Sabina had reminded her, that she'd met handsome Carson Montgomery of the rich and powerful Montgomery clan. Their brief mutual infatuation had not ended well, in large part because of the rattling skeleton in Carson's closet.

Three weeks from Saturday—that was the day she would become Mrs. John Frederick Quincannon. Now that the date had been set, invitations were ready to be sent out and other arrangements attended to—all except her selection of a wedding gown, and a decision John kept waffling on as to whom he wanted to be his best man. As for their honeymoon, a reservation had already been made at a secluded inn in the Valley of the Moon . . .

Enough daydreaming. There was business to attend to—a report on her investigation of a series of shopliftings that had plagued the White House and City of Paris dry goods emporiums. It had taken her just three days to spot the pair of young women, working in tandem, who were responsible for the thefts, track them to a Folsom Street apartment, and there recover most of the stolen items.

She consigned the scrap of notepaper and altered business card to the wastebasket, put a Carpenter and Quincannon, Professional Detective Services letterhead on her blotter, and reached again for her pen.

Outside, a Market Street trolley car came rumbling up from the Ferry Building, followed by a much louder noise, stutteringly explosive, that drowned out the trolley's clanging bell and clattering passage. Sabina didn't have to look out the window to tell that the din had been created by a horseless carriage. You saw more and more of the rackety things on the city's streets these days, tearing along at speeds up to twenty miles per hour, frightening pedestrians and animals with their tailpipe eruptions. It wouldn't be long after the new century arrived in two years, she predicted, before motorcars replaced horse-drawn conveyances as the primary method of transportation. John, who disliked change, chafed at the idea, but it didn't disturb her. Progress was inevitable; it was pointless to not accept its benefits and disregard its drawbacks.

She dipped her pen into the ink jar and wrote the report in duplicate, one copy for each of the gentlemen at the White House and the City of Paris who had joined together to seek her services. She had just finished enveloping the reports when John returned. The Seth Thomas wall clock gave the time as a few minutes before three.

She said, smiling, "Rather a long luncheon, my dear," as he shed his derby and Chesterfield.

"Yes, but we didn't dine until one o'clock. I stopped at the bank on the way back."

"How was the fare at the Olympic Club?"

"I can't say. Mr. Hoxley ordered for the table—barley soup and vegetable salad. His idea of a healthy meal, not mine or the other gent's—James O'Hearn, superintendent of the Monarch Mine."

"A productive meeting, was it?"

John rubbed at the scar tissue on his left ear. "Very productive."

"You were offered an assignment?"

"Yes. A lucrative one."

"To do what?"

He touched his ear again, then fluffed his beard. Something was weighing on his mind; she could tell by the indulgence in his habitual gestures, his slightly distracted mien. "Undercover work," he said.

"What sort of undercover work? Something to do with the Monarch Mine?"

"Yes. It's one of Hoxley and Associates' largest and most profitable holdings."

"Located where?"

He crossed to his desk before answering, taking out his briar pipe and tobacco pouch on the way. Definitely something on his mind. Sabina had a sudden feeling it was something she would not be pleased to learn.

"Near a settlement called Patch Creek, northeast of Marysville," he said when he was seated.

"What sort of trouble are they having?"

He packed and fired his pipe. "A gang of high-graders has been systematically looting the mine," he said between puffs. "Neither Hoxley nor O'Hearn has any idea of how it's being done or exactly who the thieves are, but O'Hearn has a notion that an outsider named Yost may be involved."

"What makes him think so?"

"No specific reason, other than Yost has shown up in Patch Creek three times in the past month, claiming to be a representative of a newly formed organization called the Far West Mine Workers Union but not doing much in the way of recruiting. Mostly he plays stud poker and drinks with the miners, the rest of the time keeping to himself. His most recent arrival was two days ago—not on union business this time, so he claims, but with an alleged interest in buying land in the area."

"That seems a rather flimsy cause for suspicion."

"Perhaps. Mine bosses are always leery of union men and their motives."

"So Mr. Hoxley wants you to travel to the gold camp and investigate the high-grading."

"In the guise of a hardrock miner, yes."

"John . . ."

"Yes, I know," he said, "not an easy imposture to carry off. But it can be managed."

"When would you have to leave?"

"As soon as possible. Tonight or tomorrow morning."

Sabina's own suspicions were fully aroused now. She said coolly, "It sounds as though it will be a lengthy undertaking."

"Not necessarily."

"But likely, given the circumstances."

"The financial reward is considerable—a guaranteed per diem fee, plus all expenses and a substantial bonus upon successful completion."

"Guaranteed fee for how long?"

"Ah, one month."

"And we're to be married in three weeks. Or have you forgotten?"

"Of course I haven't forgotten—"

"But you accepted the assignment nonetheless."

"I did, but—"

"Without consulting with me first."

"I wanted to, and I would have if Hoxley hadn't demanded an immediate answer. I had to make a swift decision—"

"And of course you opted for the considerable financial reward."

"It was not an easy choice, believe me. I agonized over it."

"Bosh. Will you ever get over your lust for Mammon?"

"You wound me deeply, my dear. A fair wage for services rendered can hardly be called a lust for Mammon."

Sabina bit back more harsh words; it would have been like flinging them at a stone wall. She released a sighing breath. "Have it your way, John."

"Was I wrong in thinking you wouldn't be upset at the possibility of a brief postponement?"

Now there was a disingenuous statement if ever she'd heard one. "Well, I'm certainly not pleased at the prospect. Neither will Callie be."

"But invitations haven't yet been sent out, have they? Or catering arrangements made that can't be changed? It isn't as if the wedding is to be one of your cousin's elaborate affairs . . ."

Sabina said nothing.

"Evidently I was wrong and you are upset. I apologize, truly. If you object to a potential delay, I will notify Mr. Hoxley that I've changed my mind and we'll proceed with the wedding as planned."

Oh, drat the man! He sounded contrite and appeared a trifle hangdog . . . shamming? No. John had his faults, heaven knew, but devious deception was not one of them, at least not in his relations with her. If she insisted, he would do as he'd said and cancel his acceptance, but it was plain that he wanted the job, and that he was loath to disappoint a man of Everett Hoxley's stature and influence. His agreement to the undercover assignment cast no reflection on his love for her or his desire for the marriage; it was entirely a matter of professional ego and a need if not a lust for the almighty dollar. So she wouldn't insist. She had to admit she was more miffed at not having been consulted than at the likelihood of a brief delay in their nuptials.

She said, "I won't object, on one condition. Your solemn promise that if you haven't brought the matter to a close at the end of one month, you won't try to wheedle more time on Mr. Hoxley's payroll."

"If I can't put an end to the gold stealing in a month, I'll eat my hat and yours too on our wedding day. My reputation as a blue-chip detective demands swift and complete success."

"Then I have your promise?"

"You do. And I would rather die than willingly break it."

A feeling of tenderness banished the last of her pique. She had no doubt that he meant what he'd just said—more proof, as if she needed any, of his devotion to her.

3

QUINCANNON

The settlement of Patch Creek, in the northeastern Mother Lode, was not an easy place to get to. It took nearly twelve hours—passage by ferry to Oakland, one train to Sacramento and another to Marysville, then an hour-and-a-half stage ride into the foothills in an old coach with squeaky axles and butt-sprung seat cushions. It was seven o'clock when Quincannon finally reached Patch Creek, stiff and sore and in no mood to be trifled with. The fact that he was wearing rough miner's clothing, one of three such outfits purchased yesterday in San Francisco (for the cost of which Everett Hoxley would reimburse him), added to his discomfort and his crusty disposition.

He had spent considerable time in various mining settlements over the years, including recent visits to Grass Valley, Nevada City, Jamestown, and Tuttletown. If Patch Creek were the last to draw him for a long while he would count himself fortunate. There was little difference among them other than location and size. All were rowdy, noisy, often violent places, peopled by rough-and-tumble hardrock miners and those individuals who made legal and illegal livings off of them and their needs and vices.

At first sight by starlight and lantern glow, Patch Creek was no exception. Relatively small, about the size of Tuttletown in the southern Mother Lode where he'd recovered a large sum of gold bullion stolen from an allegedly burglarproof safe belonging to the Sierra Railway. The settlement had been built on the upper flank of a canyon, in two sections connected by a bridge spanning the wide stream that gave it its name. Shacks and lodging houses were scattered along the hill on the near side, most of them the high, narrow type common to mining camps—weather-beaten, constructed in close packs, lamplight glowing palely in many of the windows. The business district stretched at a short upward angle on the far side.

The Monarch Mine and its outbuildings stood farther uphill to the south; a sky-stain of lights, both electric and lantern, marked their location. So did the steady throb and pound of the stamp mill where the gold-bearing ore was crushed and separated, the faintly luminous mounds of white tailings, the whistle of a hoisting engine. The Monarch, like most large and profitable mines, operated around the clock.

The stage rattled across the railed bridge and onto the crowded business street—Canyon Street, according to a somewhat lopsided signpost nailed to one of the bridge supports. It took up four blocks of Canyon and most of the streets immediately parallel to it on either side, a jumble of stores, eating places, and the usual assortment of saloons, eateries, Chinese laundries, and parlor houses. More noise hammered at Quincannon as the stage climbed uphill—the tinny beat of music from the garishly lighted saloons, the rumble of wagons, the cries of animals, and the raucous shouts of men. Horses, ore and dray wagons, and private rigs rattled along the street; the boardwalks were crowded with off-shift miners and other pedestrians.

The driver finally brought the rattletrap conveyance to a halt in the creekside yard of a stage and freighting depot. Quincannon alighted with the other two passengers, both mining men and fortunately uncommunicative on the long ride. He stretched the kinks out of cramped muscles, then claimed his war bag.

The stage driver directed him to Miners Lodging House #4. It was on the far side of the bridge, naturally, but only a short distance uphill—a fairly new structure that contained a dozen or more sparsely furnished rooms, each not much larger than a cell. O'Hearn had arranged one for him; he claimed it, but only long enough to stow his war bag under the bunk bed. He was as hungry as he was tired, and he felt the need to get the lay of the town at close quarters.

He was on his own here, with no one other than O'Hearn privy to his true identity and purpose. The mine superintendent had suggested apprising Patch Creek's sheriff, Micah Calder, but Quincannon had refused. For one thing, experience had taught him that small-town lawmen were not always either as honest or as closemouthed as they appeared to be. For another, O'Hearn had admitted under questioning that Calder, while trustworthy, was only a step or two removed from being dimwitted. Undercover work of this sort was a tricky business;

the fewer people who knew about it, the safer and more effective he would be.

He stopped at the nearest eating house, filled the hole in his stomach with overcooked eggs, biscuits, and lumpy gravy, and then found his way to the Golden Dollar Saloon. This, according to O'Hearn, was one of the Monarch Mine crew's favorite watering holes and thus where the alleged union representative, Jedediah Yost, could most often be found.

It was a noisy, smoke-filled, lantern-lit place without frills of any kind. A thick layer of sawdust littered with cigarette and cigar butts coated the floor. The long bar consisted of heavy planks laid atop a row of beer kegs; the mirror behind it was cracked and pitted in several places. Faro, chuck-a-luck, and poker layouts stretched along one wall, all of them drawing heavy play.

Quincannon insinuated himself among the crowd of men lining the bar. Miners tended to be clannish, and a newcomer to their ranks not quickly accepted. They were also a hard-drinking lot when off-shift, and as such leery of one who would not wrap himself around so much as a single glass of beer. Quincannon had no intention of compromising his long-held sobriety, so in order to explain his abstemiousness he manufactured a gastric ulcer in a grumbling, profane complaint that he voiced to the Golden Dollar bartender and others within earshot. This, coupled with a friendly, easygoing manner and a recitation of one of his favorite bawdy stories, stood him in good stead with the group he infiltrated. One hardrock man, a grizzled Irishman with a powder-burned chin, even expressed sympathy.

"I had a bad stomach a while back myself," he said in a mild brogue. "Couldn't drink whiskey nor even beer for a year. Worst year of me life."

"Worst three and a half of mine," Quincannon said.

"Well, now. You've already been hired at the Monarch, have ye?"

"Not yet, but I was told there's a need for hardrock men and I'd have no trouble signing on with a word put in on my behalf."

"Like as not ye won't. Who put the word in for ye, if you don't mind my asking?"

Quincannon and O'Hearn had prepared a plausible explanation at their Olympic Club meeting. "One of the bosses where I worked in Grass Valley who knows the superintendent here," he said. "His brother's a friend of mine and got him to do it as a favor."

"Which outfit in Grass Valley?"

"The Empire."

"A big operation, that. Why'd ye leave?"

"I was there two years and ready for a change. And my friend said the wages are better at the Monarch."

"Aye, the wages are good if a man carries his weight."

"I'll carry mine well enough. Always have."

"What was your job at the Empire?"

"Timberman."

The Irishman's seamed face split into a broad grin. "Well, hallelujah. So happens I'm head of a timber crew and we're among the shorthanded. Barnes is my name, Pat Barnes."

"J. F. Quinn," Quincannon said. "I was told the Monarch works three rotating shifts. Which is yours?"

"Day shift, at present. Eight to four. That suit you?"

"It does." The day shift was the one he'd requested of O'Hearn.

"Report to the paymaster's office no later than seven-thirty on the morrow," Barnes said, "and tell him I asked for ye on my crew. Meantime I'll have a talk with Walrus Ben, get his approval."

"Walrus Ben?"

"Ben Tremayne, the shift boss. You'll see why the Walrus moniker when you meet him."

"I'm grateful to you, Mr. Barnes."

"Call me Pat. You go by J. F.?"

"John to my friends and fellows."

"Give me a good day's work, John, and I expect we'll get along fine. Even if ye are a poor lad who can't be taking a drop of the creature along with the rest of us."

Jedediah Yost was not in attendance on this night. Quincannon stayed long enough to learn that, O'Hearn having given him a description of the man. Just as well. He wanted as much background information on Yost as could be obtained before devoting time and energy to investigating the man's presence in Patch Creek. Sabina would gather it as quickly as possible from the Far West Mine Workers Union and other sources, and supply it to him by coded wire.

He asked no questions of Pat Barnes or anyone else about the union man, nor did he make mention of the high-grading rumors; there was nothing that would arouse suspicion more quickly among hardrock men than a stranger showing too keen an interest in local matters. Time enough for probing once he was established at the Monarch. Now it behooved him to gain acceptance among the miners, which he'd already made inroads in doing at the Golden Dollar, and to keep his eyes and ears open and his mouth shut except when asked about his work history and indulging in the usual miners' badinage.

It was after eleven when he returned to the lodging house for a few hours' rest of his own.

The buildings of the Monarch Mine were step-laddered down the steep hillside below the main shaft, so that from a distance they resembled a single multilevel structure inside a wire-fenced and guarded compound. Their sheet metal roofs glistened under the early morning sunlight. So did the fan of tailings below the stamp mill, spread out from the foot of a cantilevered tramway that extended to the mill from the tunnel above. Jets of smoke and steam spewed out through the mill's roof stacks, fouling the air and laying a gray haze over the clear blue sky.

Quincannon rode up to the compound in one of the wagons that carried mine workers to and from Patch Creek. As early as it was, the mine yard was a noisy hive of activity. Powder blasts deep inside the mine added rumbling echoes to the din; so did a tramway skip clanging out of the main shaft and dumping its load of ore into bins set beneath the gallows frame. Three burly freight-haulers were profanely unloading materiel from a big, yellow-painted Studebaker wagon drawn by a team of dray horses. Topmen and mules maneuvered planks and heavy shoring timbers for lowering to the eleven-hundred- and twelve-hundred-foot levels currently being mined. Rope-men and track-laying steelmen were also at their tasks. Day-shift miners stood talking and laughing in little groups near the gallows frame, waiting to take the place of the graveyard-shift crew.

He made his way to the paymaster's office, as per instructions. When he gave the J. F. Quinn name, the paymaster made the damnfool mistake of saying, "Oh, right, Mr. O'Hearn said you'd be signing on." To forestall any mention of already being marked for assignment to the day shift, he quickly related Pat Barnes's request that he be put on the Irishman's timber crew. The paymaster told him to report to Walrus Ben Tremayne for approval.

Another man in the office, this one in miner's garb, had overheard the mention of O'Hearn's name. He fixed Quincannon with a long speculative look, then followed him outside.

"Just a minute, Quinn. How do you happen to know Mr. O'Hearn?"

"Who's asking?"

"Frank McClellan. Assistant foreman."

Quincannon sized him up. Thirtyish, curly-haired, thin-lipped, eyes closely set; a small jagged scar narrowed the outer corner of the left eye. A steady imbiber of John Barleycorn, if the odor of whiskey on his breath this early in the day was any indication. His manner was aggressively self-important—assistant foreman was a cushy job, mostly that of inspection of completed work—yet also wary and a little nervous.

"Well? Answer my question."

"I wouldn't know Mr. O'Hearn from Adam's off ox."

"Then why'd he tell the paymaster you'd be signing on?"

"Ask him."

"I'm asking you."

Quincannon shrugged. "A friend in Grass Valley put in a word for me here, not that it matters. I'm no damn company informer, if that's what's bothering you."

McClellan's jaw tightened. He opened his mouth, then seemed to think better of what he'd been about to say and snapped it shut again. He turned on his heel and stalked off.

A man to watch, Quincannon thought. The wariness and nervous suspicion might be due to a concern that excessive drinking would cost him his job, but it might also be apprehension if he were one of the high-graders. An assistant foreman had full knowledge of the workings of a gold mine and a free run of its gold-bearing innards.

Quincannon returned to the gallows frame just as the whistle blew to announce the end of the graveyard shift. One of the waiting hardrock men pointed out Walrus Ben Tremayne to him. A squat, beetle-browed gent of some fifty years, the day-shift boss sported thick, flowing, nicotine-stained mustaches—no doubt the source of his moniker.

Tremayne looked him up and down, grunted, and said in a wheezy baritone, "Timberman, eh?"

"That's right. Pat Barnes asked that I be put on his short-handed crew."

"So he told me. New hires usually start with the mucking crew on the graveyard shift."

Quincannon had no desire for that kind of work. Mucking meant cleaning up debris in the galleries and crosscuts after blasting—the miners' equivalent of a stablehand's backbreaking job. He said, "I came here for timber work."

"And you think you're good at it, do you?"

"I know I am. Never had a complaint yet."

"Last worked the Empire in Grass Valley?"

"For two years. A string of other mines in Sonora and Jamestown before that—all timber jobs."

Walrus Ben grunted again. "All right, then. I'll give you a chance to prove yourself down on twelve-hundred today. Tell Barnes I said so."

Quincannon sought out Pat Barnes, who showed his broad grin again and followed it with a friendly thump on the shoulder. He hoped the jovial Irishman would not turn out to be one of the high-graders. It irked him when a favorable first impression of a person proved to be false.

Inside the gallows frame the shaft cage rattled, then shot into view at a jolting, close-to-unsafe speed before squealing brakes gripped the cable. This was evidently a regular and dangerous little game played by the hoist tender, judging from the ominous grumblings among the night-shift men as they filed out, caked with dust and sweat and smelling like mine mules, and from a sharp reprimand from Walrus Ben as he led the day-shift miners onto the swaying cage.

The rebuke had little enough impact on the tender; the drop into darkness was fast and jerky, the square of light above vanishing almost immediately, for the shaft was crooked from the pressure of the earth against it. The cage bounced to a stop at the eleven-hundred-foot level, where a dozen men alighted, then dropped to the gallery station at twelve-hundred. By then Quincannon's ears were clogged and he was deaf from the change in air pressure. It was a phenomenon he hadn't gotten used to in the

Eastern mine where he worked in his youth, and likely wouldn't here, either. He stamped his feet as he stepped out, as did the others, until the pressure eased and hearing returned.

In the powder room across the station they hung up coats, stowed lunch pails (Quincannon's had been prepared for him by the cook at the lodging house), gathered tools, and lit oil-wick cap lamps and tin hand lanterns. When they emerged, Pat Barnes introduced Quincannon to the other members of his timber crew.

The graveyard-shift powder man had blasted loose tons of rock to widen and lengthen a new crosscut, and the damp, humid air was thick with silica dust and the stench of burnt powder. The job hadn't been done to Walrus Ben's satisfaction, however. Tremayne had evidently been a powder man himself prior to his promotion to shift boss; he had his own ideas on the finer points of loading, capping, and detonating sticks of dynamite, and still worked at the task, as a length of Bickford fuse visible in his coat pocket attested. He bellowed orders and gave the muckers, trammers, and timbermen not a moment's rest after they set to work.

And long, arduous work it was. It had been a while since Quincannon had engaged in heavy physical labor; it didn't take long for the carrying and setting of lumber for shoring the walls of the crosscut—and those of a new stope, a vertical shaft above the cut that would connect twelve-hundred with eleven-hundred—to blister his hands inside heavy gloves, strain every muscle, cake his freebooter's beard with dust and sweat. He was by no means soft, but mining labor put even the hardiest of men to the test, the more so one who had not in many years worked an eight-hour shift in the dangerous bowels of the earth. Down here, cave-ins, premature detonations, fires, floods, rock gas, runaway cages and tramcars were potentially greater threats to his longevity than the actions of a gang of gold thieves.

He learned nothing about the high-grading during the long shift, either by observation or listening to conversations among his fellow laborers, but he hadn't expected to his first day on the job. Or down here in the hole for that matter, at least initially. Considerably more time was needed to learn who was involved and how the gold was being smuggled out, and he had the feeling that some of the answers were to be found in Patch Creek.

4

SABINA

The day John departed for Patch Creek she arranged to have lunch with Callie, to tell her the wedding date would have to be postponed. The restaurant she chose was a favorite of her cousin's, the Sun Dial on Geary Street—a calculated and probably futile effort to provide a convivial atmosphere for the telling. Sabina was not looking forward to the task.

When she left Carpenter and Quincannon, Professional Detective Services, she stopped at the nearby Western Union office to send a wire, at John's request. It was to the headquarters of the Far West Mine Workers Union in Sacramento, asking for general background information on FWMWU representative Jedediah Yost; the reason she gave for the request was a routine insurance matter. The day being Friday, neither she nor John expected a reply until Monday.

Callie was already seated in the Sun Dial's bright, airy main dining room when Sabina arrived. Sunlight slanting through one of the large skylights laid a golden sheen on her cousin's intricately braided and coiled blond hair. On the chair beside her was one of the many lavishly fashionable hats she owned, a creation decorated with bunches of dark red currants that matched the color of her outfit and trimmed with a tall peacock feather.

In her youth Callie had been a vivacious beauty, and despite the addition of several pounds—she had an inordinate fondness for sweets—she was still regally attractive in her mid-forties. Like Sabina, she had been born in Chicago, but her family had moved to California when she was five, before Sabina was born. They had resided in Oakland for a time, settling in San Francisco when her father was promoted to the regional headquarters of the Miners Bank. Her marriage to Hugh French, a protégé of her father's who eventually became the bank's president, had firmly entrenched her among the city's social elite.

She had been delighted when Sabina moved to San Francisco from Denver, and even more delighted when she learned of John's marriage proposal and Sabina's acceptance. But today, as expected, she was anything but delighted at the news of the delay and the reason for it.

"Oh, Sabina," she said, "how could you let John take on such a lengthy assignment *now*?"

"I couldn't very well stop him."

"But virtually at the last minute . . ."

"Three weeks is not the last minute, Callie. There's still plenty of time to reschedule." Sabina paused. "You haven't already sent out the invitations, have you?"

"No. But I was about to have them printed."

"Then all that's necessary is to change the date."

"Once we know what the new date is."

"It won't be far off. John gave me his solemn promise that if he can't finish the job within the allotted month, he won't ask for an extension."

Callie said portentously, "Assuming he survives that long. Dangerous undercover work in a gold mine, of all things!"

"He has survived more hazardous undertakings." Such as the near-fatal shooting that robbed him of his earlobe, but she banished that thought as quickly as it came. "He simply can't resist a challenge or an attractive fee."

"Surely you tried to talk him out of it?"

"Yes, but he had already agreed, and his word is his bond."

"Agreed without consulting with you?"

Sabina repeated John's explanation for that.

"Humph."

A white-jacketed waiter delivered their luncheon orders—crab-and-prawn salads and crusty sourdough bread. Callie poked reflectively at one of the large prawns in her salad. "You know," she said at length, "there is one thing you could do, but I hope you're not foolish enough to do it."

"Now there's an enigmatic statement. What could I do that you hope I don't?"

"Travel to Patch Creek yourself. Keep a close eye on John instead of waiting and worrying here."

"What makes you think I'm worrying about him? He only just left."

"I know you, dear. You can't fool me by pretending you're not concerned about the welfare of the man you're about to marry."

"Concerned, yes, but not unduly. And certainly not enough

to hie myself off to Patch Creek. John wouldn't like it, for one thing. And for another, the sudden arrival of an unescorted woman in a gold camp would cause undue attention."

"You went to Grass Valley not long ago in the guise of a lady gambler."

"With John's consent and in consort with him, and that adventure nearly cost me my life. This is an entirely different situation."

"Yes, of course it is," Callie agreed with a sigh. "It's a foolish notion and I'm relieved that you find it so. I shouldn't have mentioned it in the first place."

Foolish indeed, Sabina thought. Of course she couldn't travel to Patch Creek. The only women other than lady gamblers who went to such rough-and-ready towns were saloon girls and cheap prostitutes, and she was not about to resurrect the bawdy Saint Louis Rose. Plus, there was little or nothing she could do there to assist John's investigation; her presence might even compromise it. He would never forgive her for meddling without just cause.

Sabina speared and ate a section of crabmeat, then switched the conversational topic back to the wedding.

The rest of that day and the weekend passed slowly. Saturday afternoon, after half a day at the agency, she spent shopping. She visited three exclusive women's apparel shops in an effort to select her wedding dress, but the only one that appealed to her—a taffeta gown with a fitted empire-style bodice, dropped waist, and pleated ruffles—was too fancy for what would be a relatively simple ceremony, and its pure white color was inappropriate for a widow marrying for the second time. Two more hours were devoted to a stroll through the open-air California Market, the city's block-square "entrepôt of foods," where she bought fresh fruit, vegetables, seafood for herself, and a small amount of codfish for Adam and Eve, the cats' favorite treat.

Solitary evenings at her Russian Hill flat, which she usually looked forward to, seemed to have temporarily lost some of their allure. A feeling of being at loose ends was the cause, she supposed. The flat had been her home since arriving in San Francisco, a comfortable three rooms and bath, and she would miss it, at least for a while, when she moved in with John after the wedding. His Leavenworth Street flat was larger, with plenty of room for her belongings, and though there were alterations that needed to be made—the removal, to which he'd agreed, of certain items he'd accumulated during his uninhibited bachelorhood—she was certain she would be perfectly content living there. So would Adam and Eve, eventually; cats were adaptable creatures.

On Sunday she indulged in one of her favorite activities, riding in the park with Amity Wellman and other members of the Golden Gate Ladies Bicycle Club. Amity, like her, was a "New Woman," the term used to describe the modern woman who broke with the traditional role of wife and mother by working outside the home; Amity was also an even more ardent suffragist than Sabina, head of the most active local organization, Voting Rights for Women. They had become good friends as a result of their mutual passions and Sabina's solution to a series of deadly threats to Amity's life. Sabina told her of the probable wedding postponement, Amity having agreed to be her matron of honor, and explained the reason for it. Unlike Callie, she was not critical of John's decision or Sabina's acceptance of it.

In terms of business, Monday was another dull day. No prospective clients at the office, no calls through the Telephone Exchange, no mail of any importance. And no answering wire as yet from the Far West Mine Workers Union office in Sacramento. Evidently the FWMWU was too busy or did not consider her request for information on Jedediah Yost important enough for a swift response.

She passed time by writing letters to slow-paying clients, responding to correspondence of a minor nature, reorganizing files, sifting through the wanted posters John accumulated, and finally delving into recent issues of the *Police Gazette*, a publication Callie considered unfit reading matter for ladies of culture and refinement. Sabina found that attitude amusing, given the fact that her cousin's taste in reading ran to such women's magazines as the *Ladies' Home Journal* and the moribund *Godey's Lady's Book.*

She hoped that the lack of business did not mean the agency was about to experience one of its protracted slack periods. That would make the wait for John's safe return even more difficult. What she needed was an investigation of her own to pursue, one such as the department stores' shoplifting case, that tested her detective skills . . .

Ask, and sometimes ye shall receive.

At ten o'clock Tuesday morning, a potential client arrived at the agency in the person of a young woman named Gretchen Kantor. And what she brought developed into a complicated investigative challenge, though it did not start out that way.

5

SABINA

"I hope coming here is the right thing to do," Miss Kantor said nervously from her forward-leaning perch on one of the client chairs. "But what happened was so odd, and Vernon was in such a dither about it, I . . . well, the incident really should be investigated."

"Vernon?"

"Vernon Purifoy." Then, proudly if irrelevantly, "He's very handsome. And he has an important job—chief accountant for the Hollowell Manufacturing Company."

"May I ask your relationship with Mr. Purifoy?"

The young woman colored slightly. "We have been keeping company the past three months."

And would go on doing so, if she had her way. There was a stardust gleam in Gretchen Kantor's eye, a determined set to her wide mouth and slender jaw. Timidity somewhat overcome by a strong attraction to Mr. Purifoy. She was in her late twenties,

Sabina judged, moderately attractive in an angular way. Hazel eyes and long chestnut tresses were her best features. Her gray bombazine dress and lacy white shirtwaist were fairly new but not expensively tailored, likely a product of the Maiden Lane dressmaking shop where she was employed as a sales clerk.

Sabina asked, "Were you present when this incident took place?"

"Yes. Vernon had just returned from a short business trip to Sacramento, and he . . ." Miss Kantor colored again, a near-scarlet blush this time. "He invited me to his house . . . well, actually it's a charming little cottage . . . for a homecoming celebration, you see."

"Homecoming celebration." A euphemism if Sabina had ever heard one, not that Miss Kantor's love life was any concern of hers. She asked, "What happened exactly?"

"A man was just leaving the cottage, a fat little bald-headed man Vernon had never seen before. Through the front door, bold as you please."

"A thief?"

"No, and that is what's so odd about it. Vernon was so angry I thought he was going to strike the man. He literally dragged him inside his study to see if his desk had been broken into, but it hadn't. Vernon searched him anyway. The man hadn't stolen a single thing."

"What was his explanation for having illegally entered the house?"

"He claimed he hadn't entered it, that it only looked from the street as if he were coming out. He swore he was a salesman, and I must say he was very convincing."

"Was the door to the house locked?"

"It was. But he had a ring of keys and Vernon found one that unlocked his door. The man claimed that that was just a fluke, that the key wasn't a . . . what did he call it . . ."

"Skeleton key?"

"Yes. It wasn't a skeleton key, he said. Vernon didn't believe him, and he certainly could have been inside, but for what reason?"

Sabina could think of at least two, but she didn't voice them just yet. "What did he claim to be selling?"

Miss Kantor opened her beaded handbag and produced a business card, which she handed to Sabina. It was a rather ornate card made of heavy white vellum, with curlicue borders and embossed lettering.

OSCAR FOLLENSBEE
OFFICIAL AGENT
EXCELSIOR HOME IMPROVEMENT COMPANY

"Vernon has never heard of the Excelsior Home Improvement Company," Miss Kantor said, "and neither have I. There is no listing for it in the City Directory."

Sabina said, "It's unfamiliar to me, too. What sort of business did Oscar Follensbee claim it to be?"

"A newly formed one that refurbishes older homes for nominal fees. Vernon's cottage was built in the 1870s, you see. He inherited it from his parents."

"Is it in need of refurbishing?"

"Well . . . to some extent, I suppose." The young woman

added defensively, "Vernon is very frugal, you see. He doesn't believe in spending money on what he calls nonessentials."

Sabina asked, "When did this incident happen?"

"Sunday afternoon."

"What did Mr. Purifoy do after he determined nothing had been stolen?"

"He let the man go. What else could he have done?"

"Held him and sent for the police."

"Vernon said there was no point in it since nothing was missing, that they would just view it as a misunderstanding."

"Not necessarily," Sabina said. "Not if Oscar Follensbee has a police record for burglary or illegal trespass."

Miss Kantor nibbled at her lower lip. "But if he is a criminal, why hadn't he stolen anything?"

"Perhaps he didn't have time. He may have just entered and seen you and Mr. Purifoy arriving. Or he could have been doing what is known in underworld parlance as 'casing the premises' to determine if there was anything of value worth taking at a later time."

"Yes, I see what you mean. If the man is a criminal, he may still be a danger."

"Does Mr. Purifoy keep money or other valuables in his desk?"

"I don't know. If he does, it must be just a little money. He lives very, um, frugally."

"That being the case, Miss Kantor, why did he change his mind?"

"Change his mind? I don't understand."

"You said he let Oscar Follensbee go without summoning the

police because nothing had been stolen. Why does he now want the matter investigated?"

"Oh, he doesn't. I mean, he doesn't know. Coming here was my idea, you see."

And it had taken her two days to work up the courage to do so. Sabina chastised herself for not suspecting this sooner. She'd been too eager at the prospect of a new case, not that that was a valid excuse. She suppressed a sigh. "I wish you had told me that when you first arrived, Miss Kantor. I'm afraid I can't help you."

"But . . . but why not? Surely you can find out who this man Follensbee is—"

"Possibly. But that isn't the reason I can't help you."

Miss Kantor looked as though she might burst into tears. One hand fumbled in her bag, came out with a thin sheaf of greenbacks. "This is all the money I have saved, fifty dollars, I thought it would be enough—"

Sabina said gently, "It isn't a matter of finance, but one of legal and professional ethics. We are unable to conduct investigations for private individuals other than the person directly involved or one acting as that person's representative."

"But I am acting on Vernon's behalf—"

"Yes, but without his knowledge or consent."

"You . . . you mean he has to be the one to hire you?"

"Yes. In person or by signed letter."

Two large tears squeezed out of the misty hazel eyes. "He won't agree to that, I know he won't. He j-just wants to let the matter drop."

Sabina let a sigh come out this time. "I'm sorry, Miss Kantor. Without Mr. Purifoy's authorization, there is nothing I can do."

It was not until Gretchen Kantor had made a dejected exit that Sabina, feeling somewhat dejected herself, noticed that Oscar Follensbee's business card was still on her desk blotter. She looked at it again, then picked it up. There was something vaguely familiar about it—not the wording; possibly the design. But she couldn't quite place what it was.

Well, no matter. She slid the card into her desk drawer, on the unlikely chance that Miss Kantor could convince the frugal Mr. Purifoy to change his mind, and promptly forgot about it.

She would soon have forgotten the entire matter if it hadn't been jarred back into the forefront of her mind on Wednesday morning. It was Mr. Vernon Purifoy himself who did the jarring.

He strutted into the agency not long after her arrival, stood for a moment looking around, then fixed her with an unfriendly eye and announced himself. Gretchen Kantor may have considered him handsome, but Sabina silently begged to differ. He was some four inches shy of six feet, slender in an underfed way—his dapper black broadcloth suit made him look hipless—and the owner of a mustache that spanned his upper lip in a thin, curving line and quivered now with indignation. A large but ordinary signet ring adorned the third finger of his right hand. The polished hickory walking stick he carried was an affectation, she judged, not a necessity.

"You are Mrs. Carpenter, I presume," he said. His voice was surprisingly deep for a man of his stature.

"You presume correctly."

"I have come to verify that you have no intention of investigating the incident at my home on Sunday."

"Not without your contractual permission, no."

"Which I emphatically do not give. It was a minor misunderstanding best left forgotten, as I thought I had made clear to Miss Kantor. The silly woman had no right to discuss it with you or anyone else."

"Silly woman." Evidently Purifoy did not share the young woman's romantic infatuation. He struck Sabina as a martinet, the sort of vain man whose devotion was reserved strictly for himself.

She said coolly, "That may well be true, but she did so out of concern for you and your welfare."

"Perhaps, but that is of no consequence," Purifoy said. "She is merely an acquaintance who should have known better. I do not care to have my private life invaded."

"Invaded?"

"By the police and certainly not by a female private detective. I place a high value on my privacy."

"Indeed you must."

"Then you will honor your refusal to Miss Kantor and not meddle in my affairs?"

"I have already said so, Mr. Purifoy. Would you like me to put it in writing?"

The sarcasm was lost on him. He said, "That won't be necessary. I shall take you at your word." He tapped the ferrule of his stick on the floor as if for emphasis, turned on his heel, and removed himself from her sight.

Sabina sat simmering. Everything about Vernon Purifoy

rankled, not the least of which was his cheeky, hidebound reference to her being a *female* private detective. A martinet, a prig, a denigrator of women . . . and perhaps something even more unpleasant, too? His sudden arrival in person and his insistence that no investigation be undertaken seemed out of proportion to what he himself had termed "a minor misunderstanding." In her experience that sort of heavy-handed protest meant the individual had something to hide.

Sabina seldom acted on a whim. Almost never, in fact. She was much too practical a businesswoman to allow personal feelings to overrule her judgment. But she surprised herself by giving in to impulse not once but several times over the next few days.

The first time was not long after Vernon Purifoy's visit. The day being warm, she walked up Market to Geary during the noon hour and ate her lunch at a bakery shop that served the best muffins in the city. The choice was not quite random, for the bakery was near Maiden Lane, and when she emerged she found herself detouring in that direction. She had no good reason to stop in at the Clark Dressmaking Shop, other than the fact that she felt sorry for Gretchen Kantor. There was nothing she could say to the young woman of her dislike of Vernon Purifoy, and it would be cruel to reveal the man's coldly insulting remarks about her, but there was no harm in reassuring her that she had done nothing wrong in attempting to act as his benefactor.

A whim, pure and simple.

But it became more than that when she entered the shop. It was small and somewhat cramped with display racks of inexpensive women's apparel and accessories of the sort that clerks, secretaries, and sales girls such as Miss Kantor herself could afford. There were no customers at present, and it took a few moments before a curtain parted at the rear and Miss Kantor emerged wearing a tentative smile.

That was not all she exhibited, however. A bandage three inches long stretched across her left cheekbone. The skin along its edges was discolored beneath an application of powder, the rest of her face pale.

She came to an abrupt standstill when she recognized Sabina. Something like fright showed in the hazel eyes. "Oh," she said, "Mrs. Carpenter. I . . . I didn't expect to see you again . . ."

"What happened to your face, Miss Kantor?"

One hand lifted to the bandage, lowered again without touching it. "It . . . it's nothing, really, just a small cut. I tripped and fell in my room last night, struck the edge of a table."

She was lying, covering up. It was in her voice, the quick side-shift of her gaze, the slight tremor of her hand.

Sabina kept silent. If she gave voice to what she was thinking, it would accomplish nothing. The girl would only deny that it had been the signet ring Vernon Purifoy wore, not a table edge, that had opened the wound in her cheek.

Miss Kantor said, "You haven't changed your mind, have you? That's not why you're here?"

"No, it's not."

"Then . . . ? I mean, this isn't your sort of dress shop, surely . . ."

"I just wanted to reassure you that you did nothing wrong in confiding in me yesterday."

"Oh, but I did. It was foolish of me to go against Vernon's wishes. I had no right to do that."

Virtually the same words Purifoy had spoken to Sabina, which she had no intention of mentioning. "I take it you told him of our conversation," she said, "and he has no desire for an investigation."

"None whatsoever. No."

"Why is he so adamant against it?"

"He . . . he doesn't want anyone meddling in his affairs. He values his privacy."

More parroting, Sabina guessed. Part of an angry lecture delivered by Purifoy and punctuated and bolstered by violence.

"Please honor his wishes, Mrs. Carpenter. And please don't come to see me anymore. I . . . we just want to be left alone."

Sabina took her leave, and anger rode with her on her return to Carpenter and Quincannon, Professional Detective Services. She despised men who mistreated women; verbal abuse was bad enough, physical abuse intolerable. And poor Gretchen Kantor was a prime example of a bully's victim. Her infatuation with Vernon Purifoy was so great that she forgave being struck in a fit of rage, her fear not of more abuse but of being cast out of his life.

Sabina understood both types all too well, but what she didn't understand was Purifoy's motives in this particular instance. He was a martinet and a bully, yes, but she was even more convinced now that there had to be more to his intensely negative reaction to the thought of an investigation than a desire for privacy. The apparent breaching of his home by a stranger was one part of it—or was Oscar Follensbee, if that was his real name, not a stranger at all? Another might be fear that something he kept in his desk had been stolen. Money? More than one man who lived frugally and mistrusted banks had been known to hoard greenbacks or specie.

She might not have dwelt on the conundrum if there had been agency business to attend to. But there was still none—no calls, no visitors, no mail—and the combination of boredom and curiosity was proving compelling. Of course there was nothing she could do about it legally. And yet, if one wanted to stretch a point, there was a certain moral responsibility involved. Did she want to stretch the point? Perhaps, if there was a way to do it that did not openly violate professional ethics.

Well, there was nothing wrong with conducting a private investigation, was there? Just for her own satisfaction, if nothing else?

She talked herself into it. Her second whim, this one not so pure and not so simple.

6

SABINA

On Thursday morning, shortly after she arrived at the agency, a Western Union messenger brought her a belated reply from the Far West Mine Workers Union office in Sacramento. The wire stated that the FWMWU had no record of an employee by the name of Jedediah Yost, past or present. Nor had the organization sanctioned visits to Patch Creek by any of their representatives.

Just who was Jedediah Yost, then? It might be possible to find out from the description of the man James O'Hearn had given to John, though there was little enough to distinguish him. Yost was in his late forties, of average height, slender and wiry; other than a small triangular birthmark on his left cheek and a bootlace mustache, he evidently possessed the sort of bland countenance that would render him unnoticed in a crowd of more noteworthy men. His only known habits were the smoking of short-six cigars in an amber holder and a fondness for and skill in stud poker. Sabina sifted through the agency's file of dossiers on known criminals. None matched the description or had a record of involvement in any kind of gold theft or swindle.

She hurried out to the telegraph office, where she intended to send a coded wire to J. F. Quinn, John's alias in Patch Creek, informing him that Yost was posing as a union man. The intention was thwarted, however, when she was told that Patch Creek did not have a Western Union office; the nearest was in Marysville. Telegrams could be delivered from there to the gold camp, but not without the recipient's address or a prior arrangement as to where it could be picked up. If John had known beforehand where he would be quartered, he hadn't confided the fact to her.

Drat! She should have considered that Patch Creek would be too small to have a Western Union office. So should John have, for that matter. Both had promised to exchange brief wires, she with background data on Jedediah Yost, he to inform her of his progress and reassure her regarding his welfare. Now neither was possible.

What was she to do? John would surely want the information on Yost, but how could she get it to him? And was it vital? Perhaps not. Yost was already under suspicion in the high-grading scheme; John surely would be keeping an eye on him.

Still, there might well be something in the impostor's true identity that had a bearing on John's investigation. It behooved her to do all she could to find out who and what the man was.

She paid a visit to the San Francisco branch of the Pinkerton Detective Agency, where she provided the agent in charge with Yost's description and possible criminal enterprise. The Pinkertons, as she well knew from her time as a Denver "Pink

Rose," had a far more extensive file of known felons than any other small agency such as theirs. But the branch's files contained no leads to Yost's identity.

Calls at two more of Carpenter and Quincannon, Professional Detective Service's rival investigative agencies proved equally unproductive.

There was one other possible source of information on the impostor, but she was reluctant to explore it. It was slim at best, and it would open up old wounds.

As a young metallurgist Carson Montgomery had been briefly mixed up in a scheme to steal gold from a Mother Lode mine, the Gold King, by falsifying reports on the amount and value of its gold-bearing ore. He had backed out before actually committing the crime, but his brief involvement with the conspirators, who were later caught, tried, and convicted, had led to a vicious blackmail attempt by one of them upon release from prison. The revelation of Carson's checkered past and her subsequent entanglement with the extortionist were not the only reasons she and Carson had parted ways, but they had played a significant role.

It was unlikely, given the fact that ten years had passed since the Gold King cabal, that the man calling himself Jedediah Yost would have been involved in it or that he would be known to Carson. It had been more than a year since she'd last seen Carson, and she had no desire to renew their acquaintance. He surely felt the same way. Still, as awkward as a meeting with him might be, she decided professional necessity outweighed personal feelings. So she girded herself after leaving *The Morning Call*, proceeded to the Montgomery Block, and called at the offices of Monarch Engineering (no connection to the Monarch Mine, merely a coincidental appellation).

Only Carson was not there. And the officious clerk she spoke to refused to tell her where he could be reached or when he was expected back in the office. Leave a message asking him to contact her as soon as possible? For all she knew he might be out of town, and if he wasn't, she could hardly blame him if he chose to ignore the request.

She departed without giving the snooty clerk her card. She would simply have to come back again on the morrow, on the chance that Carson would be here then and willing to talk to her.

7

QUINCANNON

It took him most of a week to put together a partial list of suspects. The Monarch's nervous assistant foreman, Frank McClellan, was one; another was a slab-faced day-shift station tender named Joe Simcox, whom Quincannon had spied sneaking away from the station one afternoon and who had unaccountably managed to disappear when followed. He agreed with O'Hearn's estimate that it would take at least half a dozen miners to steal enough gold to make the risk worthwhile for all concerned, some of whom figured to be working the night and graveyard shifts. The gang's methods were clever and sophisticated, which to him meant that it must be gold dust and not gold-bearing ore that was being smuggled out. But he had yet to uncover a clue as to how such a bold refining process could be accomplished in a mine operating with mostly full crews twenty-four hours a day.

Jedediah Yost, if in fact that was his true name, was also on the suspect list; O'Hearn had been right in not trusting the man's recurring presence in Patch Creek. Whether or not Yost was a union representative was still open to question, though Quincannon doubted it. That the camp did not have a telegraph office, a fact he had discovered to his chagrin the evening after his arrival, made it difficult if not impossible for Sabina to forward any data she might have uncovered about the man. (And for him to keep his promise to contact her periodically.) It was conceivable that Yost was an outside member of the gang, perhaps even the ringleader—the man to whom the stolen gold was given for safekeeping or for conversion into greenbacks or bonds. Deeply involved in any event.

Other factors made Quincannon reasonably sure of this. On more than one occasion, he'd learned by hearsay, McClellan had visited Yost in his room at the Monarch Hotel, ostensibly to discuss union business. Simcox had also been a visitor. To make the connection complete, Quincannon had twice seen the trio sharing a poker table at the Golden Dollar, and on another occasion spotted Yost and McClellan engaged in a low-voiced conversation that struck him as conspiratorial.

Most genuine union organizers were firebrands, but Yost was neither bombastic nor prepossessing; for the most part his manner was as bland as his countenance. According to hearsay, his call for larger wages and better safety regulations on his previous two visits had been low-key, and O'Hearn's instructions to his guards to use force if Yost attempted to enter the Monarch compound had failed to stir Yost to action. On this third stay, he had spent no time passing out leaflets and speechifying on behalf of the Far West Mine Workers Union. All of which pointed to the man's not being who and what he claimed to be.

His alleged interest in buying land in the area appeared bogus, too, since he seldom left the settlement during the day and spent most of his nights playing stud poker. Why was he here, then? Two possibilities, separate or in conjunction. One: dissension among the gang members required his presence as unifying force or peacemaker. Two: a large amount of looted gold was being stockpiled and he had come to collect it.

Just who was Yost? Gambler, grifter, professional thief, black-marketeer? And where had he come from? None of the miners or tradespeople seemed to know. Or to care, as long as he kept buying free drinks and losing as much as he won at stud poker.

Quincannon had made no effort to speak to the man directly. Nothing would have been gained by making himself known to Yost, and might have succeeded only in putting his undercover status at risk and compromising his investigation. As it was, McClellan's apparent suspicion of him as a company spy had surely been communicated to Yost and the other members of the gang. In which case they would be keeping an eye on him, just as he was doing on the three suspected conspirators.

That was one reason he had not attempted a search of Yost's hotel room, much as he would have liked to. Not for the stolen gold—Yost was too smart to keep any among his belongings—but for some idea of who the man was and where he'd come from. Such a venture was too dangerous even if an opportunity had presented itself. A newly hired timberman had no business in the Monarch Hotel unless invited, and trying to sneak in under cover of darkness was a fool's gambit.

But there was another search he could make, so long as he went about it with extreme caution. And he would, as soon as circumstances favored it.

One thing he now knew for sure was that Yost, despite his small stature and quiet demeanor, possessed a commanding presence and a penchant for deadly violence. An incident Quincannon had observed in the Golden Dollar on Wednesday night removed any doubt of that.

It happened during a game of five-card stud in which Yost was one of five players; the others were day-shift miners, Simcox but not McClellan among them. A small group had formed to watch the action and Quincannon joined them, keeping in the background.

The stakes were relatively low—one-dollar limit, maximum of two raises—but at that a fair amount of money was being won and lost. Yost had accumulated the largest pile of chips, betting conservatively and no doubt skillfully bluffing when the opportunity presented itself. He held his hole cards close to his chest, studying the cards turned faceup on the table and the faces of his opponents with sharp-eyed concentration.

Conversation was desultory, Yost contributing little to what was said, until one of the other players, a burly and half-drunk French Canadian named DuBois who had been losing steadily, turned sullen and glowering. When his nine-high straight was beaten by Yost's jacks full, and Yost allowed as how it was his lucky night as he raked in the pot, DuBois slammed a meaty fist down on the table. "By damn," he grumbled in a whiskey-thick voice, "if I don't know better I think maybe you make your own luck, m'sieu."

Yost said mildly, "But you do know better, don't you, Frenchy."

"Yah, maybe I don't. You win every time you deal the cards."

"Are you calling me a cheat?"

DuBois's lip curled. He said angrily, *"J'en ai plein le cul!"*

"You want to cuss me," Yost said, laying his hands flat on the table, "by God do it in English."

"Bah! I am sick of losing to you, that's what I say."

"Then quit playing and walk away."

"What if I don't want to quit, eh?"

"Then shut up and take your losses like a man."

Beet-red anger suffused DuBois's jowly face. He bounced to his feet, kicking his chair over backward. "No one tells DuBois to shut up!" He stabbed a horny finger at Yost and took two steps around the table toward him. Two steps only. Then he stopped dead still, because he was looking down the muzzle of a hammerless .32-caliber pocket pistol.

The weapon seemed to appear in Yost's hand as if by a conjuring trick; Quincannon had never seen a faster, smoother draw. The other poker players and the onlookers sucked in their breaths.

"Take one more step," Yost said, "and you'll be a cripple for the rest of your life."

DuBois didn't move. No one else moved either. The sudden tension was palpable; even the piano player ceased his discordant music-making. Yost meant what he'd said. Though his expression remained as bland as ever, his purpose was plain in the way he stood, the rigid extension of the gun, his unblinking gaze. The pupils of his eyes were so dark they looked black in the lamplight, as hard and shiny as anthracite.

He let several seconds pass before he said, "I won't stand for verbal threats or physical assault, Frenchy. You understand that now, don't you." The last sentence was not a question.

DuBois's anger had deserted him. He looked confused, chastened. "Yah, I understand."

"All right, then. You have two choices. Sit down and play cards, or cash in and walk out. Which is it to be?"

It took the French Canadian less than five seconds to make a decision. He pocketed his few remaining chips, saved as much face as he could by glaring at Yost, and stomped out. Only when DuBois was gone did Yost relax and repocket his pistol in a motion almost as swift and deft as his draw.

"Okay, gents," he said to the other players, his voice mild again, "we'll continue with our friendly game. Whose deal is it?"

Oh, yes, Quincannon thought, a dangerous and violent man. And an adversary not to be underestimated.

8

QUINCANNON

Like it or not, the time had come to report to James O'Hearn. The mine superintendent had demanded an early progress report, and Quincannon could not keep putting it off. After his shift ended on Friday, he contrived to remain in the mine yard after the other crewmen had departed by helping the night-shift topmen unload a shipment of board lumber and stack it in one of the long timber ricks. When he was sure all the night-shift miners had gone into the hole, he made his way to the mine office, where O'Hearn, by his own admission, could be found well into the evening.

Not this evening, however. A clerk informed him that Mr. O'Hearn had gone down to the stamp mill. The mill suited Quincannon's purpose well enough, or would as long as O'Hearn was available for a private conversation in or near its confines.

A dynamite explosion deep inside the mine made the ground

tremble as he descended a steep flight of stairs to the mill. When he entered he had no difficulty locating O'Hearn; together with an ox of a man, probably the mill foreman, he was inspecting one of the eccentrics that raised the stamps, shut down now and locked into place. Quincannon stayed where he was near the entrance, unconsciously fingering his mutilated ear and watching the machinery and the millhands at their work.

The iron-shod stamps, loosely held vertically in framed sets of five, were lifted by cams on a horizontal rotating shaft. As the cam moved from under the stamp, it dropped into the ore below and crushed the rock; the lifting process was then repeated at the next pass of the cam. Smaller pieces of ore that came tumbling down the chute went through a three-inch grizzly, or grating, into feed bins; anything larger was shunted into a jaw crusher. The dressed ore was fed automatically to the stamps.

Quincannon waited ten minutes in the lantern-lit enclosure, keeping out of the way of the sweating millhands, before O'Hearn and the foreman finished their inspection and the superintendent turned toward the entrance. His bearded face remained impassive when he spied Quincannon. He gestured that they go outside, where they could make themselves heard above the thunder of the stamps at work.

Once there and certain they were alone, he said through a glower, "Why haven't you reported to me before this, Quincannon?"

"Nothing definite to report. And the only feasible place to meet is your office or elsewhere in the compound, a tricky proposition."

"I suppose you've made no progress at all, then."

"An incorrect supposition. I have made progress."

"You know who's doing the high-grading?"

"I have an idea who some of them are."

"Well? Who?"

"I'd rather not say just yet."

O'Hearn's glower deepened. "Why the devil not?"

"I never make accusations until I have proof. I thought I made that clear to you and Mr. Hoxley."

"Dammit, man, I don't like being kept in the dark."

"You won't be for long, I promise you that."

"What about that union agitator, Yost? Is he involved?"

"I'll tell you this much," Quincannon said. "Yost is no more a union recruiter than I am."

"The hell you say. Are you sure of that?"

"Sure enough."

"What is he, then?"

"That remains to be learned."

"But he is mixed up in the high-grading?"

"That also remains to be learned."

O'Hearn emitted one of his grizzly growls. "Trying to get straight answers out of you is like trying to eat soup with a fork. You had better not be giving me a runaround, Quincannon."

"I'm not. Why would I?"

"For all I know you've sold out and thrown in with the gang—"

Quincannon's hackles rose at that. "Bah! You'll never meet a more honest man, or a better detective."

"So you keep claiming. You'd damn well better prove it if you know what's good for you."

"I don't take kindly to threats, Mr. O'Hearn, from anyone, including my employers and their minions. When you hear from me again, it will be with proof in hand."

Quincannon turned on his heel and stomped back up the stairs without a backward glance.

Frank McClellan's shack was larger and somewhat better built than the other miners' dwellings staggered along the hillside above Patch Creek. Elderberry and chokecherry bushes crowded around it, giving it more privacy than most of its neighbors and making it easier for Quincannon to approach it without being seen.

It was a few minutes before midnight now, the cold mountain night moonless, the shadows a deep velvety black. Lamplight showed in a few of the other shacks, but none of those were close to McClellan's. His was a completely dark, looming shape. The assistant foreman had been sharing a bottle of forty-rod whiskey with three others in the Golden Dollar when Quincannon left, and judging by their boisterous conversation, they intended to remain there for quite some time.

Keeping to clots of shadow, Quincannon eased up to the shack. He had armed himself tonight with the hideout weapon he favored for undercover work such as this Monarch business, and that he'd kept secreted in a pouch inside his war bag—a Remington double-barrel .41-caliber rimfire derringer. Not that he expected to need it, but he felt more secure with it close to hand.

He paused at the door to listen; the only sounds came from

a distance, wind-carried snatches of saloon piano music and the distant throb of the stamps. There was a large padlock on the door latch, fairly new by the feel of it and its staple, but it presented no problem. He had come prepared with his burglar's set of lock picks, which he'd also kept secreted in his war bag. It took him less than five minutes to breach the lock.

He left it hanging open in its hasp, parted the door from the jamb, eased himself inside, and shut it quickly behind him. The sharp odors of unwashed clothing, wood smoke, and alcohol set him to breathing through his mouth. The darkness was stygian; he struck a match to orient himself, shielding its flame with his hand. One large room, slightly less monastic than a monk's cell. Sheet-iron stove, puncheon table, wall bench, pole bunk with a thick mattress and woolen blankets. The only window was covered by a thick muslin curtain. He crossed to it, made sure the curtain fit tight to the frame by propping the shack's only chair against its lower edge.

From his coat pocket he took the other item he'd brought with him, a miner's candle appropriated from the mine stores. Searching by candlelight was no easy chore, but it was the only method open to him; his oil-wick cap lamp cast too bright a light even with the window curtain secured. He struck a match to light the candle's wick. In its glow he spied a tin dish on the wall bench; a residue of wax identified it as a candleholder. He wax-anchored the candle in the dish, then set quickly to business.

Two items were wedged beneath the bunk, McClellan's duffel and a small leather case. He examined the case first. Its only contents were three identical dark brown bottles; the label on one he lifted out bore a steel-engraved photograph of a healthy-looking, muscle-flexing gent and the words "Perry Davis' Pain Killer." Quincannon was familiar with the product—a patent medicine that claimed to have great thaumaturgic powers, good for man and beast, but whose main ingredient was pure alcohol. It was more potent, in fact, than most lawfully manufactured whiskeys. McClellan evidently did as much private drinking here as he did publicly in the Golden Dollar.

Quincannon turned his attention to the duffel and its contents. Wads of soiled shirts, socks, and union suits. A new, sealed deck of playing cards. A torn dime novel featuring the exploits of a Wild West character named Deadwood Dick. And a leather drawstring pouch. But the pouch turned out to be a disappointment. All it contained was a collar button, a woman's corset stay, two Indian Head pennies, the nib of a pen, and half a dozen other odds and ends of value only to the assistant foreman.

Quincannon replaced the pouch and the rest of the items, pushed the duffel and the case of Pain Killer back under the bunk. He searched the bunk itself, feeling under the mattress; all he found was the desiccated remains of a large moth. The wall bench yielded nothing, either; nor did the stove's ash box and flue. The woodbox beside the stove was partially full; he lifted out the sticks of firewood, to no avail. Then he moved the empty box aside to probe underneath.

Ah! A foot-long section of floorboard there was loose.

He pried it up with the aid of his pocket knife. Tucked into the narrow opening beneath was a drawstring pouch similar to the one in the duffel. This one, however, contained paydirt—literally. McClellan's private stash. Quincannon emptied a little of the gold dust into the palm of his hand, where it glittered wickedly in the candle flame. After a moment he sifted it back inside, then hefted the pouch. Perhaps two troy ounces, he judged.

He returned the pouch to the hidey-hole, covered it with the loose board, covered that with the woodbox, and restacked the cordwood inside. Then he removed the candle from the tin dish, set the dish back on the bench where he'd found it, and slid the propped chair away from the window curtain. A quick glance around assured him that everything was now as it had been when he entered. He blew out the candle flame, cracked the door open, peeked out. A night owl had the area to itself, and flew off hooting when Quincannon emerged and slipped away downhill among the shadows, feeling well pleased with the night's effort.

Two troy ounces of gold were worth less than $50 total. Not enough to prove conclusively that McClellan was one of the high-graders, but enough to satisfy himself of the man's complicity. What other reasonable explanation could there be for a mine official paid in greenbacks and coins to possess a hidden stash of pure gold dust?

9

SABINA

It did not take Sabina long to locate the man who had called himself Oscar Follensbee.

The business card Gretchen Kantor had given her was what made the task much simpler than she'd anticipated. Another study of it stirred her memory: it was familiar because another card made of the same heavy white vellum and with a similar design had been presented by an agency client within the past year or so. She rummaged through their file of business cards. Yes, there it was. Philip Justice, Importer of Fine Cigars. She recalled the case: John had exposed the individual, a disgruntled former employee, behind an attempt to extort money from Justice by dint of a false claim of marital infidelity.

The card gave Justice's business address on Battery Street but no telephone number. The importer was on the Exchange, however; a check of John's report of the investigation provided the number. And a call to an obliging Mr. Justice elicited the name of the firm that printed his business cards—Bromberg Printing and Lithographic Company.

The printer's Commercial Street address was within walking distance. Sabina closed the agency and joined the throng of downtown pedestrians. The crisp fall air was invigorating after the stuffy confines of the office; she set a brisk pace.

Bromberg Printing turned out to be a small storefront, its name neatly painted in a half-moon scroll on a plate-glass panel in the entrance door. The thump and chatter of a printing press in operation, and the usual, not unpleasant odors of ink, paper, and machine oil, greeted her when she stepped inside.

There were no customers at present, and no one behind the service counter. A hand bell on the countertop gave out a surprisingly loud ring when she struck it with her palm. Presently a middle-aged man wearing a full-length leather apron appeared. He bore a somewhat startling resemblance to a hound dog—pouches like miniature valises under his eyes, drooping jowls, ears so large and protuberant they gave the impression of flopping when he moved. Even his smile had a faintly mournful canine quality.

"Good afternoon, madam," he said.

"Good afternoon. Are you Mr. Bromberg?"

"I am. What can I do for you? If it is stationery you're interested in, I have in stock excellent watermark bond at a special price."

"Thank you, no. Actually, I have a rather unusual request a customer of yours said you might be willing to grant."

"Yes? The customer's name?"

"Mr. Philip Justice."

"Mr. Justice, the importer of fine cigars. A long-time satisfied customer, yes."

Sabina removed the Oscar Follensbee business card from her bag, placed it on the countertop. "This must also be your work, Mr. Bromberg. The paper stock and embossed design appear similar to those on the cards you supply to Mr. Justice."

He peered at it. "It is mine," he said with a touch of pride. "Printed and designed by Nathan Bromberg. You would like such a card yourself?"

"As nice as it is, no, I'm afraid not."

"Your unusual request, then?"

Sabina adopted a beguiling tone. "Well, I thought perhaps you might be so kind as to help me locate Mr. Oscar Follensbee."

"Locate him?"

"Yes." Sabina didn't like lying, but sometimes it was necessary in a good cause. "I met him recently, and we discussed home renovation. I have decided to make use of his service. But his company is quite new and not as yet listed in the City Directory, and there is no contact information on his card. Do you happen to have Excelsior's address or his own?"

"Unfortunately I do not. Not *his* address."

"I don't quite understand."

"This card I printed together with another order. One set for the customer himself, the other, this one, as a favor for a friend."

"Oh, I see. May I ask when this was?"

"A few weeks ago," Bromberg said. "A small order. Fifty cards and fifty sheets of letterhead stationery, envelopes, and contract forms for himself. And a mere twenty-five cards for

Mr. Follensbee. Such small orders from new customers I do not forget."

"What was the customer's name?"

"Goodlove. An uncommon name, easy to remember."

"And what was his line of work? Also home improvement?"

"No. He is a real estate agent."

"Oh? Would Mr. Goodlove be a plump, bald gentleman of short stature?"

"He would. You are knowing him?"

"I think so," Sabina said. "Did he have his address put on the card you printed for him?"

A frown put deep wrinkles in Bromberg's forehead, making him look even more like a mournful hound. "He did, yes. The address . . . what was it? One minute, please."

He went away into the rear of the shop. Sabina waited slightly more than a minute before he returned. "Elmer J. Goodlove, Goodlove Real Estate, 1006 Guerrero Street. Would you like I should write it down for you?"

"That won't be necessary. Thank you very much, Mr. Bromberg."

"You are welcome." He presented her with one of his own business cards. "You will remember me, please, when you are in need of quality printing and lithographing?"

"I certainly will," Sabina said, and meant it. It would be with Mr. Bromberg she would place her order for the new Sabina Carpenter Quincannon business cards.

So Oscar Follensbee and Elmer J. Goodlove were the same man, she thought as she strolled back to Grant Avenue. A pair of aliases if he were up to some sort of chicanery, which struck her as probable. But what sort of chicanery? Assuming he had illegally entered Vernon Purifoy's cottage with a skeleton key, for what reason if not to steal something?

And why had he had two cards printed for two different businesses, home improvement and real estate? Some sort of swindle involving both? But if that were the case, why was he carrying only the Excelsior card when Purifoy caught him?

She puzzled over these questions for a full block before a notion began to take shape. Suppose the "new" home improvement business was completely bogus, nothing more than a name to back up his salesman's story if he were spotted trespassing on private property; that would explain the lack of an address on the Follensbee card, and why he hadn't been carrying the Goodlove card. In which case his game had something to do with the real estate business.

Real estate. And illegal trespass with a skeleton key.

Her memory jogged, produced a connection to a swindle she'd been told about that had been perpetrated in the city before her move here from Denver. Same dodge, same crook after a long hiatus? One thing a detective learned from experience was that anything was possible, no matter how far-fetched it might seem. That included audacious confidence games that worked because of their fantastic nature.

Elizabeth Petrie was the person who'd told her about the swindle, and since Elizabeth could usually be found at her Hyde Street residence, Sabina proceeded there directly from Market

Street. The trolley ride proved to be worthwhile: Elizabeth was home and welcoming as always.

The creation of finely crafted wholecloth and patchwork quilts was her profession, but her true passion was police work. She and her late husband, Oliver, had both been on the San Francisco force, he as an inspector and she as a matron. But when Oliver was implicated in a corruption scandal, and convicted and sentenced to Folsom Prison, the scandal's taint had unjustly robbed her of her job. Oliver had drowned himself in whiskey after his release and eventually died of acute alcoholism, but Elizabeth had persevered. In her late forties now, she supported herself not only by selling her quilts, but by working part-time for a select few of the city's private investigative agencies, Carpenter and Quincannon, Professional Detective Services being one of them, when they were in need of an experienced female operative. Her gray-haired, grandmotherly appearance combined with her no-nonsense intelligence made her a valuable asset in a wide range of cases.

Elizabeth had been blessed with a sharp memory and was a font of information on local criminal activities, particularly those that had taken place during her time as a police matron. She had shared accounts of some of the more interesting and bizarre cases with Sabina, one of them being the real estate swindle. She was eager to repeat the details once Sabina explained the reason for her visit.

"It certainly sounds like the same clever con as the one back in '89," she said. "And the same fat little bald grifter running it."

"What was his name?"

"He went by Harold Newcastle. Sure to be an alias."

"He calls himself Goodlove now, if he's the same man. Elmer J. Goodlove."

Elizabeth smiled wryly. "A particularly specious handle, that one."

"Did Newcastle make use of a second name and a second bogus business such as the Excelsior Home Improvement Company?"

"No evidence of it was found, as I recall, but I wouldn't be a bit surprised if he did. The department never did find out his real name. Or where he went after he skipped with his spoils."

"How much did he get away with?"

"Close to five thousand dollars, based on the statements of the people he swindled," Elizabeth said. As she spoke she continued to work on her current project, a handsome medallion quilt with a large Tree of Life at its center; she sewed rapidly and effortlessly, without making a stitching error or losing her train of thought. "Two officers were dispatched to his hole-in-the-wall real estate office in Polk Gulch after the first victim complaint was filed. Asa Brinkman was one of them. He was a sergeant then; now he's a lieutenant in charge of the Fraud Division. I'm sure he'd be delighted to get his hands on the man."

"Newcastle was already gone when the officers arrived?"

"Either he smelled trouble or just decided it was time to pull up stakes. The office was closed and empty of any phony transaction records he kept."

"And nothing has been heard of him or his activities since?"

"Not until now. Went on practicing his grift in other cities, no doubt, and managed to stay out of the hands of the law. A slippery cuss. You know the type, Sabina—charming, slick-talking, shrewd, and like most of his breed, as cold-blooded as a snake."

Sabina nodded; she knew the type all too well. "Refresh my memory on exactly how he worked his swindle."

"By selling property, or shares in property, he didn't own. Abandoned buildings for renovation, vacant lots for new construction. He collected down payments from the marks, mostly for alleged ninety-day escrow closings."

"Tricky business. He couldn't hope to remain in one place more than a few months."

"The secret of his success," Elizabeth said. "He must have a sixth sense about just when to close up shop and disappear. He made the mistake, or near mistake, of operating here too long in '89, in order to complete a large score on a private home he claimed had just been put on the market. The buyer was completely duped, because Newcastle or whatever his true name is gave him a tour of the home before an agreed-upon down payment was made. It was the buyer who filed the criminal complaint, after showing up at the house without Newcastle for another look around and being confronted by the owner."

"How much was the down payment?"

"Twenty-five hundred dollars. In cash."

"No small amount. Was it the victim who chose the house?"

"Yes. He was looking for a certain type of affordable home in the neighborhood."

"So what Newcastle must have done, then," Sabina said, "was to scout up a place that fit the victim's specifications."

"That's it," Elizabeth agreed. "By wandering around, observing, and asking discreet questions. The one he picked was temporarily empty, the owner and his wife being away on an extended vacation. The place had no immediate neighbors, so it was a simple matter for him to let himself in with a skeleton key and take a general inventory of the premises, which he then passed along to the victim. Once he had the mark hooked, he took him to the house for the tour."

"And did he steal anything from the home?"

"No. The owner found nothing missing when he returned."

"Just as Vernon Purifoy found nothing missing from his cottage."

"Clearly the same swindle and the same mountebank working it. He must have decided that eight years was long enough to allow him to come back here and run his swindle under a different guise in a different neighborhood. Bold as brass."

"And twice as lucky, if he has never been caught."

"I wonder how long he's been operating in the city this time."

"Five weeks or so," Sabina said, "judging by when he had the business cards and stationery printed. Long enough for a mark looking for a Potrero Hill cottage to seek him out, and for him to scout up what he considered a likely place."

"Fortunate for Mr. Purifoy that he returned home when he did and made Goodlove's first illegal entry the last."

"Not necessarily the last."

"Oh? Do you expect him to try again despite being caught in the act?"

"He might be persuaded to, yes."

Elizabeth paused in her stitching. "That sounds as though you intend to try persuading him."

"I'm thinking of it."

"But why?"

Sabina hadn't confided her dislike and suspicions of Vernon Purifoy; they were best kept to herself for the present. She said only, "I have my reasons."

"Well, I'm sure you know what you're doing. But my advice is to report him to Lieutenant Brinkman straightaway before he bilks any more marks and disappears again. Even without evidence of present criminal activity, he can be arrested on the old fraud charges."

Sound advice, but Sabina was not ready to take it just yet. Purifoy's oddly secretive, violent behavior nettled her enough to warrant a bold effort to get to the bottom of it. And there might be a way to accomplish that, depending on just how reckless and just how greedy the swindler was.

10

SABINA

Vernon Purifoy's address was listed in the city directory as 2675 Eighteenth Street, which put it at the foot of Potrero Hill rather than on the hill itself. Originally a Mexican land grant called Potrero Nuevo, Sabina had been told, the area had not been a convenient location to get to, separated as it was from the rest of the city by Mission Bay. It was not until the Long Bridge had been built in the mid-1860s that access to Potrero Hill was made easy enough to transform the area from a virtual wasteland into a desirable hub. In the years since, it had been settled by working-class families, many of whom toiled in the shipyards, iron factories, steel mills, and warehouses that stretched south along the bayfront between China Basin and Islais Creek Channel.

On Friday morning Sabina rode a trolley car across Long Bridge and another to Eighteenth Street to have a look at the Purifoy property. Gretchen Kantor had referred to the place as "a charming little cottage," a decidedly rose-colored-glasses view. It was in fact an early, 1870s version of Pelton's "Cheap Dwellings," named for the architect who designed them and that proliferated in the Potrero and Irish Hill neighborhoods. Built on a lot no more than twenty feet wide, it appeared to be one of the four-room variety considered modestly stylish and attractive in its day, with a scrolled, Eastlake-style front door and a heavy projecting cornice. Time and neglect had taken their toll on it. Miss Kantor's estimation that it was in need of renovation "to some extent" was another generous assessment; in fact it needed considerable work, including structural repairs, a fresh coat of paint, and a new roof.

What had made it ideal for Elmer Goodlove was that unlike many Pelton cottages, it was not one of a linked row built close to the street. Rather, it was set back a short distance behind a weedy front yard and screened from its neighbors, one a renovated and expanded Pelton, the other a brown-shingle dwelling, by clumps of unkempt shrubbery. A trespasser's access to it, if casually managed, would be sure to go unnoticed.

Satisfied, Sabina proceeded to her next stop—Goodlove Real Estate, 1006 Guerrero Street.

As expected, this turned out to be a narrow storefront—what Elizabeth had referred to as a hole-in-the-wall. Goodlove had spent a minimal amount on rental space, but the sign above the door was artfully painted in a design similar to that on the Bromberg-printed business cards. Another sign on the door, equally artful, proclaimed: **Peerless Homes and Lots for Sale.** A good confidence man of Goodlove's ilk knew when and how to put up a proper front while still minimizing his overhead.

A bell over the door tinkled musically when Sabina entered. The interior was one long room with a handful of functional furnishings—two desks, four chairs, a filing cabinet. One wall was adorned with photographs of dwellings in far better condition than Vernon Purifoy's cottage and attractive vacant lots, under which another sign boldly lied: **Purchases by Our Satisfied Clients.**

The office's only occupant had bounced up from one of the desks and hurried to greet Sabina. Elmer J. Goodlove in the flesh—short, roly-poly, with a fringe of white hair, shiny blue eyes, and skin as smooth and pink as a baby's. "A hearty good morning to you, my good woman," he said jovially, beaming. The shrewd blue eyes took immediate note of the fact that she was well dressed. "Welcome to Goodlove Real Estate. Elmer J. Goodlove, at your service. And you are?"

"Mrs. Jonathan Fredericks."

"A pleasure, Mrs. Fredericks. What can I do for you?"

"I am interested in purchasing a home not far from here."

"Indeed." The fat smile grew even fatter. "I have some excellent properties of all types, sizes, price ranges—"

Sabina said imperiously, "My interest is in a specific property, if it should happen to be for sale. There is no sign to that effect and no one answered my ring at the door. I have come to you as the nearest agent in the hope that you might know if the property is for sale."

"Splendid. Where is it located?"

"On Eighteenth Street. Number 2675, to be exact. A four-room Pelton cottage."

Goodlove, like most confidence men, was an expert at concealing surprise. "Ah," he said.

"Does that mean you are familiar with the property?"

"No, I'm afraid not. Other Pelton cottages, but not that one."

"So you cannot say if it is for sale."

"No. But I have a listing for another Pelton, as well as other, more attractive, well-constructed homes—"

"I am not interested in other Peltons or other homes of any sort. Only in that particular cottage."

"May I ask why?"

"My brother saw it on a recent visit and expressed a liking for it, despite the fact that it is in poor repair, and for the neighborhood. He is a carpenter by trade, experienced in home repair, and I am encouraging him and his wife to move to San Francisco from Santa Rosa. He hasn't much money, and I happen to be in more fortunate circumstances, so I would like to surprise him with a gift of the cottage he desires."

"A generous gesture, most generous indeed," Goodlove said. "But if I may say so, there are much more advantageous real estate investments than a Pelton—"

Sabina essayed an impatient gesture with her folded parasol. "Are you or are you not prepared to accommodate my wishes, sir?"

"Of course, most assuredly," Goodlove said hastily, "if in fact the owner is willing to sell."

"If he isn't, I expect he can be talked into it for the right price. Money, Mr. Goodlove, is no object."

"Indeed? Ah, may I ask how much you are willing to pay?"

"Whatever amount is necessary, within reason."

"As much as one thousand dollars?"

"As much as three thousand dollars," Sabina said.

Again nothing changed in Goodlove's expression, but he could not prevent a flicker of avarice from showing in the bright blue eyes. Peltons were known as "cheap dwellings" for good reason, as Sabina had discovered in her research. In the early 'eighties a three-room cottage stripped of such frills as an indoor water closet could be bought for as little as $500, while a fully equipped four-room cottage was priced at $850. Their value had appreciated somewhat in the past two decades, but considering the run-down condition of Vernon Purifoy's property, its real estate market value was hardly more than $1,000.

"Would you wish to pay the purchase price in installments?" Goodlove asked through his fat smile.

"Certainly not. My offer is an outright cash sale."

The flicker of avarice had become a steady gleam. "Well, in that case the owner should be sorely tempted."

"He would have to be a fool not to be," Sabina said. "Of course, I do have one stipulation before I commit to purchase."

"And that is?"

"That I be allowed an examination of the cottage's interior."

"For, ah, what reason?"

"To determine if any structural or other changes have been made that my brother might find objectionable."

It was a somewhat thin explanation, but Goodlove seemed not to notice. "I could ask the owner—"

"Who might not give you an honest answer. No, that won't do."

"Well . . . would it be necessary for you to be present in person? I have considerable experience in such matters, and I could examine the rooms for you and make a list of any alterations—"

"Absolutely not. I have no doubt you are qualified, but I will need to visit the premises myself. I trust you understand."

"Yes. Yes, of course."

"Then you agree to act as my agent in this matter?"

"I do. With pleasure, Mrs. Fredericks. I will attempt to meet with the owner of the property at . . . what was the address again?"

"2675 Eighteenth Street."

"Yes. To meet with the owner as soon as possible and do my very best to persuade him, or her, to sell on your terms."

"I would appreciate an answer as soon as possible," Sabina said. "Tomorrow, preferably."

He balked at that, as she had known he would. He couldn't be sure Vernon Purifoy would be away from home tomorrow. "That, ah, is very short notice. Too short, I fear. Property owners approached for an immediate sale often require time to think over an offer . . ."

"By Monday, then. That should be enough time."

"Monday. Yes. I will do everything in my power to, ah, accommodate you by then. Assuming a sale can be arranged, how soon will your brother wish to take possession? Sixty days? Ninety?"

"Thirty. The sooner he is able to move into his new home, the happier we both will be."

"Mmm, yes, I see. Very well. Step over to my desk, if you will be so good, and I shall draw up a preliminary agreement."

The agreement was of a standard, bare-bones sort, more or less legally binding if Goodlove had been a legitimate real estate agent. Sabina signed it "Mrs. Jonathan Fredericks" in a disguised hand.

He said then, "I appreciate your faith in me, Mrs. Fredericks, indeed I do. May our association be mutually beneficial." Sabina endured the moist clasp of his hand in hers. "I will try my very best to have a decision for you by Monday. Shall we meet here again at one o'clock?"

"The time is satisfactory, but I suggest we meet at the cottage. I expect the decision to be favorable, in which case I will be able to examine the interior without delay."

Goodlove hesitated for three or four heartbeats before saying, "As you wish. One p.m. Monday at the Eighteenth Street address."

Was he well enough hooked and hoodwinked by the prospect of a large amount of cash to run the risk of invading Vernon Purifoy's cottage a second time? Sabina thought he was. Purifoy lived alone and would be away at his accountant's job on Monday, so the risk was minimal and the reward considerable. The maximum figure she had named was surely too powerful a lure to resist, for he stood to collect the entire amount by simply claiming the owner refused to settle for less. Three thousand dollars was a considerable score for a small-time confidence man, even if it should mean abandoning his current setup sooner than expected.

11

SABINA

It was nearly four o'clock when Sabina exited a Market Street trolley car at the corner of New Montgomery. On weekdays, Fridays especially, this was the time when many prominent businessmen young and old left their offices early to embark on the Cocktail Route—a daily round of upper-class watering holes such as the Reception Saloon, Hacquette's Palace of Art, and the Palace Hotel Bar that for some lasted well into the night. Business deals were made, political alliances formed, schemes hatched over drinks and lavish free lunches. And for more than a few of the silk-hatted gentry, married as well as single, the evening's bacchanal ended in one of the fancy Uptown Tenderloin parlor houses run by such as Lettie Carew and Miss Bessie Hall, the notorious "Queen of O'Farrell Street."

Carson Montgomery had not been a Cocktail Route habitué when Sabina was keeping company with him, but for all she knew he had succumbed to its temptations since she'd last seen him in the Palace Hotel's Grand Court a year and a half ago. Recently his name had been linked with a socially prominent Crocker family debutante, a liaison reported in more than one newspaper's society column, but that did not necessarily mean he was ready to give up his bachelor's lifestyle. She really didn't know him all that well.

Her second venture to his Montgomery Block suite proved, unlike her first, to be successful. The same officious clerk she had spoken to previously admitted that Carson was present but attempted to deny her an audience with him by once again stating that an appointment was required. She was not having any of his annoying attitude this time. She handed him one of her business cards and, in the same imperious tone she had used on Elmer Goodlove, demanded that he deliver it to his employer immediately. Her profession, if not her name, raised an eyebrow and ended any further argument. He went away with the card, returned in less than a minute, stated much more politely that Mr. Montgomery would see her, and pointed the way to Carson's private office.

Sabina hadn't been sure how she would feel when she saw Carson again, and was mildly relieved to feel nothing at all. Not even a twinge of regret. On their first meeting at Callie's dinner party, she had found him strikingly handsome—eyes as blue, kind, and gentle as Stephen's, long sideburns, curly brown hair, warm smile—and when she'd looked into those bright blue eyes she had been instantly smitten. Now, it was as if she were in the company of a man who had never been anything more to her than a casual acquaintance.

If he still had feelings for her, any pangs of regret, they

were not apparent. His smile was tentative and puzzled as he came forward to briefly take her hand in his. He said a trifle awkwardly, “It’s good to see you again, Sabina. You’re looking well.”

“As are you, Carson.”

He cleared his throat. “I understand you and your partner are soon to be married. My sincere congratulations.”

“Thank you.”

“Surely you haven’t come to invite me to the wedding.”

She chose to let the remark pass without comment. She said, “A business matter you may or may not be able to help me with. Frankly I’m not at all comfortable talking to you about this, but I’ve run out of other possible sources of information.”

“What makes you uncomfortable? Our former relationship and how it ended? That’s all in the past now, Sabina.”

“Yes, but the questions I have involve the past—yours, not ours.”

“My past?” His smile faded into a puckered frown. “You’re not referring to the Gold King conspiracy?”

“I don’t believe so. Indirectly, if at all.”

“Regarding a matter your firm is investigating?”

“That John is investigating, yes. An organized high-grading operation at a gold mine in the northern Mother Lode.”

“Oh, Lord. You can’t possibly think I might be involved?”

“No. Of course not. My questions have to do with a man who may be one of the gang, a shadowy figure posing as a miners’ union representative under the name Jedediah Yost. I am trying to find out just who he is.”

“While your partner investigates at the mine.”

"Yes."

"And you believe I might know this man Yost, is that it?"

"Might have encountered him or heard of him during your travels in the gold country."

"That was ten years ago, Sabina."

"It's a slim possibility, I know," she said. "But I'm at the grasping-at-straws stage."

Carson's frown smoothed away. "I'll help if I can. I don't have to tell you of my animus for thieves."

No, he didn't. His near-disastrous youthful peccadillo had taught him a hard lesson. He was an intrinsically honest man, a good man. Sabina had doubted that during her investigation of the extortion attempt, but only briefly.

He invited her to sit, waited until she was seated and had removed her hat, then sat himself facing her across his desk. The desk was large, of polished mahogany—the only expensive furnishing in what was otherwise a strictly functional office. Neither Carson's wealthy family background nor his success as a mining engineer had altered his proletarian nature.

"What can you tell me about this man Yost?" he asked.

"Very little, other than a description provided by our client and the fact that he has enough knowledge of gold mining and miners to successfully pose as a union man."

"Describe him."

She did so. Carson sat quietly, his hands steepled together under his chin, while he cudgeled his memory. At some length he said, "The triangular birthmark. On his left cheek?"

"Yes."

"Ordinary-looking otherwise, and small in stature."

"Yes."

"In his middle forties . . . The age is about right," Carson said musingly. "The birthmark and the rest of the physical description, the amber cigar holder, the knowledge of gold mining, the liking for stud poker—too many similarities to be mere coincidence."

Sabina sat forward in her chair. "You know him, then?"

"There was a man in Downieville while I was there, an assayer named Morgan. Crooked as a dog's hind leg by reputation, though nothing was ever proven against him. He was also rumored to have been responsible for the death of a rival for his wife's affections."

"He sounds ruthless."

"And was, evidently. Ruthless and mercenary."

"Did you have any dealings with him?"

"Fortunately, no. Though he did make a veiled overture that I refused to listen to."

"I wonder if he still resides in Downieville."

"I'm sure he doesn't," Carson said. "Not long after I moved on, I heard that he and his wife were sent packing by the local authorities. Where they went I don't know, but his wife was from Sacramento and vocal about her desire to move back there."

"Can you recall his given name?"

"Bart."

"Short for Barton or Bartholomew?"

". . . Bartholomew, I think. Yes, Bartholomew."

"And his wife's name?"

Carson searched his memory again, shook his head. "I'm sorry, I can't recall it."

That was all he could tell her about either of the Morgans, but it was quite a bit more than she could have hoped for. They parted at the door with a friendly handshake. Neither of them expressed an interest in seeing the other in the future, however. This meeting had not been as awkward as Sabina had feared, but it hadn't been a comfortable one either, for her or for Carson. She had her life, he had his, and it would be better for both if never the twain should meet again.

Just how important to John and his investigation was the information Carson had given her?

She debated the question as she made her way back to Market Street. Important, certainly, if Bartholomew Morgan alias Jedediah Yost was mixed up in the high-grading plot, as now seemed probable. But John was shrewd and highly inquisitive; after a week of undercover work, he would surely suspect by now, perhaps even know, that Morgan was posing as a union representative and possessed a tainted past. If only she knew whether or not the man was still in Patch Creek. And if he wasn't, if John had any idea of where he could be found.

Had Morgan and his wife established themselves in Sacramento or its environs after their ejection from Downieville? Even assuming they had back in 1887, eleven years was a long span of time for a ruthless crook to remain in one place. They could have moved any number of times, together or Morgan alone if he had abandoned or divorced his wife. He might also have conducted legal and illegal business under the Yost alias or another name not his own.

The agency kept a file of city business and residential directories; she went there first and consulted the Sacramento Directory on the chance that Morgan had established an assay or metallurgy business in the capital under his own name or that of Jedediah Yost. No, he hadn't. There were several listings under both "Assayers" and "Metallurgists," but none of the names was even remotely familiar.

Well, there might be another way to find out.

At the Western Union office she composed a lengthy wire to Henry Flannery at the detective agency he operated in Sacramento. John considered Flannery reliable enough to have established a quid pro quo agreement with him some years back. She requested any available data on Bart or Bartholomew Morgan alias Jedediah Yost, formerly of Downieville, and included the detailed description and all the information Carson had supplied on Morgan's background. She marked the wire "Urgent." Assuming Flannery was not out of town on a case, she would have a preliminary response from him shortly, and another as soon as he had something to report.

12

QUINCANNON

When he dropped off the Monarch mine wagon on Saturday morning, Quincannon spied Frank McClellan among the gaggle of day-shift men waiting in the shade of the gallows frame. The slab-faced station tender, Joe Simcox, was at his side. McClellan was immediately aware of his presence as well; the assistant foreman said something to Simcox, and both men cast looks in his direction. Did the pair sense that they were under suspicion? Not a bad thing if so. It might render one or both nervous enough to make a mistake that would bring about their undoing.

Quincannon removed his miner's hat, sleeved road grit from his face. As early as it was, the day promised more Indian summer warmth, with none of the cooling winds that often blew in these Sierra Nevada foothills. Off to his right, the departing wagon raised another column of dust as it started back down the long passage to Patch Creek. Where the creek itself was visible among willows and aspens, the water caught sunlight and dazzled like molten silver.

He moved across the noisy mine yard, took up a position next to Pat Barnes, and pretended to ignore McClellan and Simcox. Soon the whistle blew and the shaft cage began its rattling ascent. As on previous mornings, the hoist engineer played his dangerous little game of bringing the cage to a jolting, squealing halt. More than one of the graveyard-shift crew cursed him on their way out, as some did every morning; the profanity only succeeded in producing a jeering grin.

Quincannon and the other day-shift men crowded into the cage. He contrived to stand next to McClellan as Walrus Ben gave two sharp pulls on the hoist cord, the signal to lower the cage. McClellan glared at him, fidgeted, then turned his back.

The plunge into the bowels of the mine rendered Quincannon deaf as usual. He stamped his feet to ease the pressure, followed the others across the station into the powder room, where he exchanged his hat for an oil-wick cap lamp. Down here on twelve-hundred the temperature was thirty or more degrees cooler than topside, and twice as damp—a cold dampness that got into and lingered in a man's bones. He hadn't gotten used to that, either, and likely wouldn't as long as he worked in the hole.

He started after Barnes and the other timbermen toward the crosscut that was being driven across a new and potentially rich vein. Before he'd cleared the station a hand caught hold of his arm from behind and drew him to a halt. McClellan. The assistant foreman's breath was redolent of the Perry Davis' Pain Killer he hoarded in his cabin, and his fox face already ran with sweat. In the smoky light from their cap lamps, his eyes held a sheen of what Quincannon took to be a mix of anger and fear.

When the other men passed out of earshot, McClellan said in a harsh whisper, "Who the hell are you, mister?"

Quincannon shrugged off his hand. "J. F. Quinn, timberman. As if you didn't know."

"I know you've been eyeballing me up here, following me down in Patch Creek. What I want to know is why."

"You've made a mistake. I've no interest in you beyond our time in this treasure hole."

"You're not a miner," McClellan said. "I know miners . . . You're too soft, too deep for this work."

"Too deep, mayhap. Hardly too soft."

"What are you after?"

"My wages, same as you."

"I think you're a damn company spy."

"Do you now? And what would you have to hide that would bring you to the attention of Mr. O'Hearn?"

McClellan clenched his teeth, stared hard for a few seconds as if at a loss for something more to say. Then he spun on his heel and clumped off into the drift. Quincannon watched him leave his sight with a feeling of satisfaction. This particular fish was well hooked and squirming. It would not be long before McClellan—and soon enough after this, his fellow thieves—was caught in the net.

The morning passed quickly. Quincannon was too busy hauling and shoring lumber to slip away, as he had done previously whenever the opportunity presented itself, for short searches of the maze of tunnels and stopes that might offer some clue to the high-grading method.

McClellan spent part of the morning on twelve-hundred, then disappeared. Gone up to eleven-hundred, or was he up to something down here? He returned toward the end of lunch break, spoke briefly to some of the men, one of them Joe Simcox, while his gaze roamed among the others. When he spied Quincannon, he looked away almost immediately. A short time later he wandered off along the drift, but not without a backward glance to see if he was being observed. Quincannon pretended great interest in the contents of his lunch pail.

The timber crew was working in the same general area that McClellan had gone. Quincannon followed Pat Barnes and two other members of the timber crew along the narrow rail track, walking on ties made slippery by an ooze of water that ran down the walls and trickled across the floor. Some distance beyond the station, the drift ran in a slight upward gradient. A tram car loaded with waste rock rattled toward them, pushed rapidly by an old-timer named Lundgren, and the group parted in a hurry. There was no sign of McClellan in the vicinity.

"Fire in the hole!"

The warning shout came from the direction of the newly driven crosscut and was quickly repeated by a number of other voices. Walrus Ben or another powder man had set a charge of dynamite that was about to be detonated. Quincannon and the others in the drift held still, covering their mouths with handkerchiefs. When the blast came, a relatively small one probably designed to remove a stubborn obstruction, Quincannon felt the rough rock floor quiver slightly beneath his boots. Soon afterward a thin mist of silica dust came rolling into the drift, briefly impairing vision until it settled.

Quincannon seized the opportunity to slip away into a narrow side turning. He would not be immediately missed by Barnes and the others, and when he was, it would be assumed he'd gone after more lumber.

Once around the turning, he was alone in the sultry gloom. He bent to reach inside the top of his right boot for his hideout derringer, slid it into a trouser pocket. It was a serious offense for an employee to bring a pistol into the mine, and he had not cleared his breach of the rules with O'Hearn. But he had a strong feeling that his investigation was coming to a head, and there was no rule made that he wouldn't breach in the interests of his own safety.

A second turning, some two hundred feet ahead, brought him into another crosscut that opened to the left and was relatively free of rock dust from the recent blast. The cut had been sealed off months ago, when the vein that ran there played out and traces of rock gas made further blasting unsafe. Once before he had seen McClellan head alone in this direction, but by the time he was able to follow, there'd been no sign of the man. Nor was there any sign of him now. He was either in the abandoned crosscut or he'd climbed one of the stopes that led up to eleven-hundred.

Quincannon paused at the boarded-up entrance to the cut. No light showed between the chinks and no sounds came from within. He examined the boards—and a small smile curved his mouth when he discovered that two had been pried loose of their fastenings and then propped back into place. By McClellan, no doubt. And there could be only one reason for the assistant foreman to venture inside an unused tunnel such as this.

Extra light was called for, Quincannon decided. He lit one of the candles he'd appropriated from the storeroom, pulled the loose boards aside and then back into place behind him as he stepped through. The air within was stale, dank, but carried no hint of gas. His cap lamp and the candlelight threw flickering shadows over walls of rock thinly veined with quartz. The cut had progressed no more than forty rods. Halfway along was the roomlike opening to an abandoned stope. He went inside, held the candle high. The stope hadn't been cut all the way through; it ended in solid rock some fifteen feet above his head.

He inspected the support timers and other possible hiding places without finding anything, then continued his examination along the walls of the cut. Thin trickles of water wet them, dripping down to collect in little puddles here and there along the base. It was in a rotting pile of scrap lumber near the unbroken face of the end wall that he found what he'd been hunting for—the method by which the high-graders were refining chunks of gold-bearing ore, and a cache of pure gold dust produced by the process.

The dust was in a small drawstring sack similar to the one he'd found in McClellan's cabin. Some twenty troy ounces, judging by its weight—several hundred dollars' worth.

The method was a small but well-constructed tube mill—a short length of capped iron pipe with a bolt for a pestle. When a piece of rich ore was dropped into the tube, a few strokes of the grinding pestle would pulverize it. The residue would then be washed out with water in a battered tin cup and the gold transferred to the sack. How the dust was being smuggled out past the shift inspectors remained to be determined.

Doubtless there were more homemade grinders hidden elsewhere on this level and eleven-hundred above. How many depended on the exact number of miners in the gang and just how much dust they were milling from pockets with a substantial accumulation of native gold. Every half spoonful of looted gold, according to O'Hearn, represented the loss of ten dollars clear profit to Hoxley and Associates.

Quincannon considered returning the sack to where he'd found it, decided confiscating it was the better course of action, and slipped it into his pocket. The tube mill was too large to fit there without detection; he returned it to its hiding place. In McClellan's present jittery state, confronting him with knowledge of it and the cache of dust might crack him open like a bad egg. Not down here in the hole, however. Topside, in a private place such as McClellan's cabin, where he could use intimidation and guile—and if necessary, force—to bring about a confession.

He made his way back to the entrance, extinguished both his oil-wick lamp and the candle before he moved the loose boards and stepped out. Thick darkness awaited him, and he heard nothing except the distant ring of sledgehammers on steel, the thump and rattle of ore carts on the tram tracks. He struck a lucifer to relight his lamp.

No sooner had the match flared than his ears picked up a faint scraping noise behind him, the unmistakable sound of a boot sole on stone. He hunched his shoulders, started to duck down and away—too late. Something solid fetched him a savage blow alongside the temple, bringing a spurt of blinding pain.

Quincannon and the match went out at the same time.

He was just lifting onto all fours, conscious again but dull-witted, when he heard the sound of the pistol shot. It jerked him upright onto his knees, set up a fierce pounding in his head. His vision was cloudy with double images; it seemed a long while before he was able to bring his eyes into focus. And when he did, he could not immediately credit what he saw in the dancing light from a kerosene lamp that had been spiked into a nearby support beam.

He had been carried or dragged back inside the abandoned crosscut to within a few feet of the unfinished stope. In front of him the body of a man lay on its back, legs inside the little room, torso and arms stretched outward. McClellan. Blood gleamed across the front of the assistant foreman's heavy-weave shirt; wide-open eyes stared sightlessly at the ceiling. On the wet floor alongside him was the Remington hideout gun.

Wincing, holding his head with one cupped hand, Quincannon used the rough wall as a fulcrum to lift himself unsteadily to his feet. He leaned there to look around, breath rattling and whistling in his throat. Except for the dead man, he was alone in the cut.

But not for long.

Noises came from the closed-off entrance—boards being yanked aside, men crowding through. A dark mass of them separated into four as they hurried forward, their cap lights throwing distorted shadows along the walls. Pat Barnes, two other timbermen, and Walrus Ben Tremayne. They drew up short when they saw what lay on the rock floor.

"Lord Almighty!" Barnes said. "It's Mr. McClellan. Dead?"

Walrus Ben hunkered beside the body. "He'll never be deader. Shot clean through the heart."

One of the timbermen said in awed tones, "Never thought I'd see the day when something like this happened down here."

"What did happen, Quinn?" Walrus Ben demanded.

"I've no answer for that yet."

"So? What were you and him doing in here?"

Quincannon said nothing this time. He wiped sweat from his forehead, trickling blood from the wound above his temple, then lowered his hand to feel his pants pocket. It was empty now, the sacked gold dust gone. He had no need to look for the tube mill to know that it had been taken, too, and either rehidden or disposed of. Hell and damn! Anger flared hot in him, driving away the last of his confusion.

Walrus Ben scooped up the derringer, peered at it in the flickering light. "And whose bloody damn weapon is this?"

There was no denying ownership. The letter Q was carved into the handle. "Mine."

"Brought down to kill poor McClellan, eh?"

"I've killed no one."

"Why were you armed, then?"

"I had good reason."

"There's no good reason for bringing a pistol into the hole.

What do you claim happened here, if not cold-blooded murder? Hard words over something, a fight?"

"I didn't kill him, I tell you," Quincannon said. "I was slugged from behind, and only just regaining my wits when I heard the shot."

"Aye, we heard it too," Barnes said. "Missed ye in the drift and come looking."

Walrus Ben said, "If you didn't fire the pistol, Quinn, who did?"

"The same man who pounded my head. But I didn't get a look at him either time."

"A bloody thin story, that. You admit ownership of the weapon. And there's no one here but you and McClellan, him dead as a doornail."

"Whoever did it must have gotten out of this cut before you arrived and escaped into a stope."

"No likelihood of that," Barnes said. "We were in sight of the entrance when the shot sounded."

"Then he's hiding somewhere nearby."

But he wasn't. Walrus Ben ordered the timbermen to examine the rest of the cut and the unfinished stope.

"There's but one way in and out of here," the shift boss said then, "and nobody alive before we came except you, Quinn. You're the slayer, no other. Confess and have done with it."

Confess and be damned for a crime I didn't commit? Quincannon thought bitterly. Faugh! But there was no gainsaying that the circumstantial evidence against him appeared conclusive—as pretty a frame as ever had been set around an innocent man. By whom? And how had the bloody deed been accomplished?

13

QUINCANNON

Quincannon had no great liking for jails, and he actively detested the one in Patch Creek. One reason was that it was the only one he had ever been locked up in as a suspect in a crime of any sort. Another was that the cell's stone walls and floor were cold, damp, unclean, and smelled about as sweet as a backyard privy. And the third was that his jailer, Micah Calder, was even more simple-minded than James O'Hearn had led him to believe.

"No, I ain't gonna send for Mr. O'Hearn," the sheriff kept saying in a voice like the scrape of a rusty pump handle. "He's an important man, he ain't got time to bother himself with a murderin' timber hauler."

Quincannon felt like strangling him; since that wasn't possible, he strangled two of the rusty bars that separated them instead. An audience with the mine superintendent would set him free of this hellhole, but nobody was willing to grant him one.

Not Walrus Ben Tremayne or Pat Barnes; they'd turned deaf ears to his pleas when they tied him up, escorted him out of the Monarch, and put him into one of the mine wagons under guard for the run to the Patch Creek jail. And not this dunderheaded lawman, half a century old and the owner of a face the approximate hue and texture of a dried chili pepper, with a brain to match.

"How many times do I have to say it?" he said. "I did not murder Frank McClellan."

"Evidence says you did. Witnesses say you did."

"There weren't any witnesses to the shooting."

"That ain't what I was told. Four witnesses say it was you done it, else you wouldn't be in here charged with a capital crime."

Quincannon pointed to his temple, wincing when his fingertip touched the weal there. "Hell, man, do you think I gave myself this knot?"

"Could have. I knew a fella once hit himself on the head with a hammer so hard he near busted his skull."

"And I'll wager I know who it was."

"Think so? Who?"

"You."

"Hey, now," Calder said in offended tones, "ain't no call for you to get personal."

Quincannon gave vent to a blistering six-jointed oath, quit strangling the bars, and flung himself down on the cell's lone cot. The fact that the mattress was as thin and hard as a slat, it and the blankets no doubt a-crawl with vermin, urged him to unleash another lengthy oath. The sheriff shook his head twice as if pained by the outbursts, then stomped out of the cellblock and locked the door after him.

Quincannon allowed himself a calming five-minute sulk, after which he commenced cudgeling his brain for an explanation to McClellan's murder. The motives for it and for the frame he found himself in were not difficult to surmise; the identity of the slayer and the methods by which he'd committed the deed and vanished afterward continued to elude him. Damnation! If only his head would stop aching long enough so he could think clearly again.

Time passed at a sluglike crawl. Calder didn't come back. The other three cells were empty; the only sounds were those that penetrated the windowless stone walls from outside. Quincannon's headache finally eased, as did most of his anger, and he resumed his brain cudgeling, this time with glimmerings of success.

The day was waning into dusk before he had company again, not the sheriff but a fat deputy bearing a tray of something resembling food. A renewed demand for an audience with O'Hearn fell on deaf ears; the deputy went away without saying a word, not even when Quincannon unleashed his frustration again in a blistering assault on the man's lineage.

Night fell. Quincannon alternately paced the cell, lay on the cot, and brooded. Where the devil was O'Hearn? He must have heard the news about McClellan by now; he should have come of his own volition. Well, it was still early. Mayhap he would.

But he didn't.

And so Quincannon spent his first and what he hoped would be his last night in durance vile.

14

SABINA

The *Morning Call*, the most reliable and least guilty of yellow journalism of the city's several newspapers, had its offices on Commercial Street. Sabina stopped in there on Saturday morning to see Ephraim Ballard, the elderly gentleman with more than forty years' journalistic experience who presided over the sheet's morgue. Sabina had met him through her acquaintance with Millie Munson, the paper's society editor, and found him always to be affably willing to demonstrate his remarkably accurate memory.

Unfortunately, he had not even a scrap of useful information to give her. The *Morning Call* had printed no news stories about the unscrupulous activities of a Downieville assayer named Bart or Bartholomew Morgan, nor was the name Jedediah Yost familiar; Ephraim double-checked the files to make sure. Whatever Morgan had been up to the past several years, he had avoided brushes with the law that were newsworthy enough to have been reported here in San Francisco.

Vernon Purifoy's name was likewise unfamiliar to Mr. Ballard. Not that that meant Purifoy was a model citizen, but merely that he had done nothing overt enough to place him in the public eye. The only thing Sabina learned from Ephraim was that Purifoy's employer, the Hollowell Manufacturing Company, was a large and profitable fabricator of chair and buggy cushion springs located on Stevenson Street, had been in business for fifteen years, and was owned by Lucas J. Hollowell and Norman A. Hollowell, father and son, president and vice president.

Waiting along with the morning mail when she arrived at the agency was a pro forma telegram from Henry Flannery, stating that he was available to oblige her request regarding Bart or Bartholomew Morgan and that he would give the matter his immediate attention. The mail contained one small and one medium-sized check, the latter in payment of a past-due invoice for services rendered, and nothing else of interest.

Just before noon Callie French paid an unexpected visit. "I thought I might find you here, Sabina. Have you had word from John?"

"No, none yet."

"Oh, dear. You must be very worried."

"Not really," Sabina said. She explained about the lack of Western Union facilities in Patch Creek.

"They must have postal service. He could have written you a letter."

"Only if he had something to report. Obviously he hasn't yet."

"Well . . . if you're not concerned, then I won't be either."

"Did you come all the way here just to ask me about John?"

"No. I'm on my way to do some shopping."

"Not for another new hat, I trust."

"Don't you like the one I'm wearing?"

Sabina didn't, particularly; it was more than a trifle ostentatious for a daytime outing, a virtual garden of violets and other flowers topped with an aigrette of lace and grosgrain ribbons. But she said tactfully, "It's very becoming."

"I may stop at a hatter's," Callie said, "but mainly I'm after a proper dress for the wedding. Have you picked out your gown yet?"

"No."

"Then it's high time you did. You don't seem busy. Close up and come along with me, and we'll see what we can find."

"I'm not in the mood for shopping."

"It's a sorry day when a woman about to be married is not in the mood for shopping." Callie studied her with a critical eye. "You know, Sabina, you really should get out more, partake of life's pleasures—you spend too much time alone. Do you have plans for tomorrow?"

"No. Why?"

"I have two tickets to an afternoon performance of Verdi's *Il Trovatore* at the Grand Opera House. Hugh refuses to go with me and I would rather not go by myself. We could have supper at Tadich Grill afterward."

Sabina was not a great admirer of opera, but she did like *Il Trovatore;* and the fare at Tadich Grill was quite good. It would be a better way to spend Sunday than bicycling in the park—the weather had turned cold and foggy—or sitting with Adam and Eve in her flat. She accepted the invitation.

Callie was right—she did spend too much time alone. Now especially, while John was away and incommunicado on a potentially dangerous assignment. Despite her denial, she *was* a little worried about him.

15

QUINCANNON

It was a few minutes shy of Sunday noon when O'Hearn finally showed up at the jail.

A key scraped in the cellblock door again and he came stomping in, Sheriff Calder trailing along behind. The mine superintendent stood glowering through the cell bars; Quincannon matched the glower with a fierce one of his own. He was in no mood for censure or harangue. He had slept poorly, his head wound still pained him, and overnight his mutilated ear had developed an annoying phantom ache.

He said before O'Hearn could speak, "I didn't kill Frank McClellan."

"He kept sayin' that when they brung him in," Calder said. "That, and demanding to see you."

"All right, Micah. You can leave us alone now."

"You sure you don't want me to stay? He's a mean one, murderin' poor Mr. McClellan the way he done—"

"I did not murder McClellan!" Quincannon shouted.

O'Hearn turned his glower on the sheriff and gestured impatiently. Calder said, "Yes, sir, Mr. O'Hearn. But you need me, you just holler."

When the cellblock door closed behind Calder, Quincannon said in a tolerable imitation of O'Hearn's grizzly growl, "Why in blazes didn't you come yesterday?"

"I was down in Marysville, that's why. Just got back and heard what happened in the mine."

So that was it. A tolerable enough excuse, though it didn't put a balm on Quincannon's temper. "You want me to proclaim my innocence again, or will you take me at my word?"

"Calder told me four witnesses swear you're the only man who could've done it."

"Bah. Four *ear* witnesses, mayhap. If they can be credited."

"If?"

"Assuming the lot of them aren't in cahoots."

"All four? A shift boss and three timbermen? That's preposterous. I've known Walrus Ben and Pat Barnes for years, and as for the others—"

"I'm not saying I believe it," Quincannon said. "What do *you* believe, Mr. O'Hearn?"

"I don't know what to believe yet. If you didn't shoot McClellan, who did?"

"Who else but one of the other high-graders."

"He was part of the gang? You're sure of that?"

"Sure enough. He knew I was on to him, and the man who shot him knew it too. Likely he was killed for fear he would turn on his partners. He was on the verge of cracking. A sharp prod or two and he would have."

"Do you have any idea who his partners are?"

"An idea, yes."

"An idea? You told me the next time I saw you you'd have proof."

"I will have, once I learn how the crime was committed."

"Dammit, Quincannon, you were hired because you have a reputation as a competent detective. How could you allow McClellan to be killed?"

"It wasn't my fault. I was taken by surprise."

"Not your fault? He was shot with *your* pistol. Why the hell did you bring a derringer into the mine?"

"For self-protection, of course."

"Hah. Didn't do you any good, did it."

Quincannon made no further effort to defend himself. The truth was, he hadn't been as careful as he should have been yesterday morning, not that he would ever admit to it. Even the keenest detective slipped up now and then, though the lapse rankled nonetheless.

"What put you on to McClellan?" O'Hearn demanded.

There was nothing to be gained now, and much to lose, by continuing to play his cards close to the vest. Without hesitation, he explained about the ties among McClellan, Simcox, and Jedediah Yost, what his search of McClellan's shack had revealed, and his discovery of the tube mill in the abandoned crosscut.

O'Hearn digested the information, and it somewhat mollified

him. "So it's dust they're taking out and tube mills they're using to grind the ore."

"Just so. But a search for the tube mills would be futile. You can bet the one I found and all the rest have been dumped into the ore chutes and destroyed by now."

"I was thinking the same thing." Then, after a pause, "Yost. I knew that bugger had to be mixed up in the high-grading."

"He may well be the ringleader," Quincannon said, "though I've found nothing yet to prove it. McClellan's murder might have sent him packing. My hope is that it didn't, that he's still in Patch Creek."

"And if he isn't?"

"I'll proceed with my investigation here and track him through his cohorts. Assuming you believe me about McClellan and can get me out of this blasted cell."

O'Hearn made up his mind. He gave his whiskers a finger raking and said, "It seems I've no choice but to give you the benefit of the doubt. But I warn you, Quincannon. Don't make a fool out of me. And you damn well better make good on your boasts."

"I intend to." Then, as O'Hearn started away, "You won't tell Calder my true identity?"

"Not unless I have to."

He went to the cellblock door, banged on it until the sheriff let him out.

Quincannon paced the cell restlessly, rubbing at his ear in a futile effort to alleviate the phantom ache. His patience had grown wafer-thin by the time O'Hearn reappeared some twenty minutes later. Calder, at his side, didn't look happy as they came down the corridor.

"I sure hope you're doing the right thing, Mr. O'Hearn," he said when they reached Quincannon's cell. "It don't seem safe, you taking responsibility for a suspected killer—"

"We've been all through that." And evidently it had been settled solely on the strength of the mine superintendent's position in the community, without any revelations having to be made. "Just get on with it."

"Yes, sir." Keys rattled and clanked as Calder unlocked the cell door. "All right, Quinn. You're sprung in Mr. O'Hearn's custody."

"And not a moment too soon."

Quincannon stepped out and the three of them trooped into the sheriff's office. He said then, "My derringer. Do I get it back?"

"Not on your tintype," Calder said. "It's evidence, that gun. I got to keep it locked up for your trial."

"There isn't going to be a trial, not with me as the defendant."

"Well, we'll see about that. You still ain't getting the murder weapon, whether you're the one fired it or not."

Quincannon started to argue, changed his mind when he saw the look on O'Hearn's bearish countenance. Instead he asked Calder, "What has been done with the remains?"

"You said which?"

"You're not hard of hearing, Sheriff. Frank McClellan's corpse. It isn't still at the Monarch, is it?"

"No, it ain't. Mine wagon brought it in."

"Where was it taken?"

"Why d'you want to know?"

"That's my business."

Calder emitted a noise like a sputtering donkey engine. "Now you look here, Quinn—"

"We're wasting time," O'Hearn snapped. "If he wants to see the body, then so do I. Where is it? Over at Hansen's?"

"Yes, sir. I guess I'd better go along, too, you don't mind."

"All right. Let's get it done."

Hansen, whoever he was, was a local entrepreneur. Four businesses occupied an adjacent pair of frame buildings just off Canyon Street, all of which bore his name—undertaking parlor, carpentry shop, gunsmith, barbershop. The undertaking parlor was at the rear of the carpentry shop, presided over by a man in a black suit whose name was Finley, not Hansen. Like Calder, he deferred to O'Hearn and offered no protest at the request to view McClellan's remains. The body was in the embalming room, already stripped of clothing. Quincannon gave it a narrow-eyed examination, but it told him nothing.

"What was done with his clothing?" he asked then.

Finley, a middle-aged beanpole with a cast eye, blinked several times as if the question confused him. "Clothing?"

"The corpse wasn't brought in naked, was it?"

"Naked? Certainly not."

"His clothing, his miner's duds. Where are they?"

"All beyond saving," Finley said. "Filthy, blood-soaked, scorched . . ."

Quincannon resisted an impulse to shake him as he would a stick.

O'Hearn's patience was even more sorely tried; he growled, "Show us the clothing or it's *you* who'll be beyond saving."

Finley wasted no more time. He led them into a storeroom of sorts and showed them the bundle, string-tied and stuffed into a trash bin, and then promptly fled. Quincannon untied the bundle, shook out the garments. The powder-marked bullet hole in the heavy-weave shirt told him that McClellan had been shot at point-blank range; the baggy trousers, undershirt, and union drawers held no clues.

He studied the high-laced boots. Along the edge and sole of the left one, and across a small section of the hooks and buckles, was an irregular, smudged black line. He rubbed a thumb over it, further smudging the black, then held the thumb to his nose and sniffed. A small satisfied smile put a crease in his freebooter's beard.

He returned the clothing and unmarked boot to the trash bin. Dangling the left one by one of its buckles, he extended it to Calder. "Keep this under lock and key, Sheriff. And make sure you carry it by the buckle."

"What for?"

"The same reason you're keeping my derringer. Evidence."

"Hell! A boot? What kind of evidence is that?"

"The kind that can hang the actual murderer."

Calder made grumbling noises, but he took the boot. O'Hearn said to him, "After you lock that up, Micah, go over to the hotel and find out if the union man, Yost, is still registered."

"Yost? What for?"

"Stop asking questions and do what I ask. We'll wait here for you."

"Yes, sir. Whatever you say."

The sheriff went out, hurrying. Once the door was shut again, O'Hearn said, "Well, Quincannon? What'd you find on that boot?"

"Black from the black deed."

"What the hell does that mean?"

"It means I'm on the right track. But more evidence is needed, and I know how to get it."

"How?"

"By going back down into the mine tomorrow morning. On my regular shift on twelve-hundred."

O'Hearn stared at him as if he'd taken leave of his senses. "The miners won't stand for you returning to work as if nothing happened today. They'll rip you to pieces."

"Not if you vouch for my innocence. You're in charge—they'll listen to you and obey your orders."

"No guarantee all of them will. They'll suspect you're a company spy, and the high-graders will know it for certain."

"Detective, not spy. And it won't matter if they know. No one outfoxes or disarms John Quincannon more than once."

"You're not thinking of taking a weapon into the hole again?"

"I am. A small-caliber pistol, fully loaded."

"By Christ, you've got gall. You're the one liable to get himself shot dead this time."

"It's a risk I'm willing to take to put an end to this business. One day, two at the most is all I'll need."

"If you live that long."

"You'll pass the word to Walrus Ben, then, and to Pat Barnes to let me back on his timber crew? And would you supply the pistol? I'd rather not chance buying one."

O'Hearn let out an exasperated breath. "More *damn* gall. All right, I'll oblige you again. But don't ask for any more favors. You're on your own starting tomorrow morning."

"When and how do I get the pistol?"

"I'll have it delivered to your room tonight after supper. Just make sure you're there to—" He didn't finish the rest of the sentence, because knuckles rattled on the door just then and the sheriff poked his dried-chili-pepper face inside.

"That fella Yost checked out of the hotel yesterday, Mr. O'Hearn. Left on the morning stage to Marysville."

Quincannon said, "Hell, damn, and blast!"

Calder blinked at the explosive response. "Something wrong in Yost leaving?"

"Never mind, Micah," O'Hearn said. "Shut the door and wait for me. I'll be right out."

"Just you? You ain't gonna leave Quinn here by his lonesome, are you? Suppose he tries to run off?"

"He won't."

"Well, if you say so . . ."

"I say so. Just remember—if anybody asks why he's not still a prisoner, you tell them to talk to me. And don't say anything about this little side trip or McClellan's boot."

Calder said, "I'll remember, yes, sir," and shut the door.

O'Hearn stayed just long enough to growl, "One day, two at the most."

It was not so much a reminder, Quincannon thought sourly, as a veiled threat.

16

QUINCANNON

On his own after leaving the undertaking parlor, Quincannon spent the rest of Sunday afternoon and evening in his room at Miners Lodging House #4, nursing his sore head, planning strategy for the morrow, and pining for Sabina. Now that the end of his investigation was in sight, he yearned to rejoin her in San Francisco, to be making renewed plans for their wedding and once again sharing a bed.

The pistol O'Hearn had procured for him, which arrived by messenger wrapped in heavy paper, was not one he would have chosen for himself. A nickel-plated Sears, Roebuck .22-caliber Defender, it could be bought for sixty-eight cents new. At least it was a seven-shot weapon and all the chambers were filled, though it would need to be fired at close quarters to do much in the way of defending.

In the morning he tucked the revolver into his right boot before going down to the dining room. Cold, mistrustful silence greeted him, and he was left to eat alone. Not that he'd expected any different. O'Hearn had kept his promise to spread the word that J. F. Quinn was considered innocent of McClellan's murder and would be returning to his work in the mine, but that didn't exonerate him in the eyes of the hardrock men. Why, they'd be asking one another, would the mine superintendent have vouched for J. F. Quinn unless he'd been a spy in their midst all along?

The morning being cool, Quincannon walked uphill to the mine instead of waiting for one of the wagons. In the yard a few of the topmen gave him hostile looks and one muttered a slanderous allusion to his masculinity, all of which he steadfastly ignored. Few of the day-shift crew had assembled yet; it was still more than an hour shy of the whistle. He crossed directly to the gallows frame, where he found Joe Simcox in conversation with the hoist tender.

"You've no right to be walking around free," Simcox said with a belligerent glare, "after what you done to Frank McClellan, much less allowed to go back down into the hole."

Quincannon paid that no heed, either. "Open the cage," he said to the hoist tender.

"Graveyard shift's still working."

"I've no intention of bothering any of them. Open the cage, if you value your job."

"Goddamn company mole," Simcox said, and spat juicily at Quincannon's feet.

Quincannon neither moved nor commented, matching Simcox's glare with one of his own. It had been many years since he had lost a staredown, and he didn't lose this one. Simcox muttered an obscenity, spat again, and turned his attention elsewhere.

The hoist tender likewise thought better of any further argument. He went ahead and opened the cage. Quincannon barely had time to lower the safety bar before the brakes were released, and the descent was no less than what he'd expected—a fast downward hurtle and a jarring stop that rattled his teeth and popped his ears. As he stepped out into the station on twelve-hundred, he saw no one in the immediate vicinity. He stomped his feet to bring back his hearing, then went to fetch and light a cap lamp.

The ring of steel against rock, shouts, and other noises told him that most of the graveyard crew was working in the new crosscut, getting ready to "tally and shoot the face"—mining parlance for the loading of drill holes with dynamite for end-of-shift blasting. He moved off quickly along the rails in the opposite direction, encountered no one on the long trek to the abandoned crosscut. As he neared it, he slowed his pace and transferred the Defender from his boot to his trouser pocket.

The loose boards had been nailed securely into place across the entrance, but it took only a brief effort with a toll pick to gain access. He went ahead to the unfinished stope, stepped inside by a pace, then squatted to wash his light over the floor. It took him less than a minute to locate what he was looking for. As he'd surmised, there had been no good reason for McClellan's murderer to have removed the object. He left it where it lay. Flimsy evidence because of its commonness in these confines, but coupled with McClellan's boot it confirmed his suspicion as to how the frame against him had been arranged. One more piece of proof was all he needed.

Distant "Fire in the hole!" warning shouts came as he emerged from the drift. He had enough time to replace the boards before the first of the end-of-shift dynamite blasts set up echoes and vibrations. He waited there until the other powder shots had been fired in sequence, then made his way back. When the whistle sounded, he was waiting behind a pile of timber for the night crew to file into the station and the cage to take them topside.

Walrus Ben Tremayne and the rest of the day shift found him in the powder room a few minutes later, readying for work. As expected, there were ominous grumblings from the men, followed by a direct verbal assault from the shift boss.

"You must be daft, Quinn, coming down here again after what you did yesterday."

"Spy for the owners," one of the other miners muttered. "Paid to get away with murder."

"Aye, and not welcome among us," Pat Barnes said, "no matter what Mr. O'Hearn says."

"I'm neither a spy nor a murderer," Quincannon said. "Innocent until proved guilty, as the superintendent believes, and here to do a day's work for a day's pay same as you."

He had banked on the fact that hardrock men valued their jobs more than they disliked and distrusted interlopers, and he was right. If the murder victim had been one of their rank and file, instead of a crew boss, they might have given him a roughing-up in spite of O'Hearn's orders. As it was, there were no further challenges and the men moved away to their various duties—all except Walrus Ben, who blocked Quincannon's way as he started to join Barnes and the other timbermen.

"You'll not do shoring in the new crosscut, Quinn," the shift boss said.

"No? Why not?"

"Because I say so. You'll work where I tell you."

"And where would that be?"

"We'll be hoisting ore on the skip this afternoon. The night-shift boss tells me there's a jam in number-four trap. You'll pull the chute."

"Dangerous job for a new man unfamiliar with the trap."

"If you don't follow orders, I have the authority to fire you for insubordination. Whether Mr. O'Hearn likes it or not."

"I didn't say I refused. There's no job I'm not up to."

"Then get to it!"

Reluctantly Quincannon made his way to the main chute, which ran at a forty-five-degree angle under the drift to two trapdoor exits in the shaft, twenty feet below the station. Smaller chutes fed the main one from above, and the muckers on the graveyard shift had shoveled into them vast amounts of ore blasted loose at the end of the night shift. Jams were common. "Pulling the chute" meant climbing down into the shaft, opening the blocked trapdoor, and by means of a long, heavy iron bar, freeing the obstruction so ore could flow freely into the skip, a coffin-shaped steel box that held six tons.

It was hot, dirty, hazardous work that required careful attention and dexterity of movement. Quincannon, standing on a plank two feet wide, poked and prodded the bar up into the chute's innards in an effort to break the jam piecemeal. If it broke all at once, and he was not quick enough to dance clear, one or more of the rocks might knock him off his perch. Just last year, he'd heard, a chute-puller on one of the upper levels had been pulverized at the bottom of the shaft.

The job went disagreeably slow. He was a novice at this kind of labor; the narrow plank was slippery and strewn with spilled ore that had accumulated and banked up. Water dripped steadily down the shaft's walls, onto his neck and down his back. The smoky flame of his lamp gave too little light. The trap seemed about to free, jammed again, freed a bit, jammed. His arms and back ached from the strain of prying, poking, pounding.

He had begun the task on his guard, but frustration and fatigue took their toll. He began to curse, even more inventively than usual, and his voice echoed loudly in the chute. So he didn't hear the man ease into the shaft on the ladder above him. If the weapon the man carried hadn't accidentally scraped against the rock wall, the last sound Quincannon ever heard would have been his own voice blistering the stale air.

The ringing noise jerked his head around and up, just in time to avoid a savage downward jab with an iron bar identical to the one he held. The assailant was the slab-faced station tender. Teeth bared, Simcox swung the bar again. Quincannon screwed his body sideways, again in the nick of time; the iron swished air past his head, clanged against rock. For an instant he lost his balance, teetered on the edge of the plank. He managed to brace himself by jamming the bar against the wall, and shoved back out of the way as Simcox's bar slashed at him a third time.

It was the station tender who was off balance then. Before Simcox could set himself for another thrust, Quincannon reached up left-handed and caught a tight grip on the end of the other's weapon. He yanked downward, hard. His intent was to pull Simcox off the ladder, send him crashing into the chute, but Simcox released his grip. When Quincannon did the same, it was the bar that dropped clattering into the jammed ore.

For an instant the two men glared at each other in the smoky light. Then Simcox's nerve broke. He twisted around, clambered out of the chute. Quincannon hauled himself up the ladder and gave chase, still clutching his bar.

When he burst through into the drift he saw Simcox fifty yards away, casting a look over his shoulder as he fled into the station. A knot of other miners stopped what they were doing to stare. Quincannon yelled, "Stop him! Stop that man!" but none of the men moved to obey.

From beyond a curve in the drift there came a rumbling that signified an oncoming tram car. Simcox didn't seem to hear it; he ran across the turning sheet, a massive plate of boiler iron where cars and skips were shunted and rotated, and onto the ties between the same set of tracks. A few seconds later the loaded car rattled into view, the old-timer, Lundgren, pushing it with his usual speed down the slight grade.

Somebody shouted, "Look out!"

Simcox heard the cry or the noise of the car or both, realized his danger in time to jump clear. But he lost his footing on the slippery floor, fell, rolled against the wall. In that same moment the car hit the switch to the turning sheet—too fast, causing the switch to malfunction. The car rocked, tilted, and then slipped sideways off the track, spilling most of its load at the point where Simcox had gone down.

The station tender's scream was choked off in the tumbling roar, and he disappeared under the crushing weight of steel and waste rock.

Lundgren and the other miners swarmed around the wreckage. Quincannon joined in the frantic scramble to unpile the rocks and lift the car, but there was no hope of rescue. Simcox's own mother would not have recognized him when what was left of him was finally uncovered.

After the remains had been shrouded, the men stood in a silent, grim-faced cluster. One gestured angrily, and when he said, "Quinn here was chasing Joe across the station just before the accident," every eye fixed on Quincannon.

Walrus Ben Tremayne stepped forward, his nicotine-stained mustaches bristling. "Two men dead in two days. Damn you, Quinn, you're a murdering menace."

"Bah. Simcox paid for his own sins. He slipped into the chute while I was breaking up the jam and tried to kill me."

"Why would he do that?"

"He was ordered to."

"The hell you say. By who?"

"By you, Tremayne."

Surprised mutterings came from the miners. Walrus Ben growled, "That's a bloody lie! Why would I give such an order?"

"Simcox was a high-grader," Quincannon said. "So was McClellan. And so are you—and a cold-blooded assassin to boot."

The muttering voices grew louder, ominous now. Miners had no tolerance for high-graders among their numbers, and the accusation that their shift boss was both a thief and a murderer heightened their natural enmity; as were most taskmasters, Tremayne was generally disliked. Sharpened gazes shifted from Quincannon to Walrus Ben and back again.

Someone said, "Can you prove what you claim, Quinn?"

"Quincannon's the name—John Quincannon, neither a miner nor a company spy but a San Francisco detective hired to investigate the high-grading. I was close to unmasking the thieves, and Walrus Ben knew it. That's why I was marked for death today, that and his attempt to lay the blame for his murder of McClellan on me."

Tremayne snapped, "*My* murder of McClellan? Another damn lie! The derringer he was shot with belongs to you, and you were alone with him in the crosscut. Nobody but you could have murdered him."

"Nobody but *you* is more like it. You shot McClellan because you knew he would crack under pressure and implicate you, and then you knocked me on the head afterward."

"How in hell could I have done that from out in the drift, in the company of three timbermen?"

Quincannon picked Pat Barnes out of the crowd and addressed him. "You were one of those with him, Pat. Why were the four of you on your way to the abandoned cut?"

Barnes said, scowling, "Ben told us there was thought of reopening it and he wanted us to inspect the support beams."

"Did you notice I wasn't with the timber crew or did he call your attention to it?"

"He did. The rest of us were too busy shoring."

"Where were you working at the time?"

"Number-four stope."

"Which direction did Tremayne come from?"

"Why . . . the direction of the abandoned cut."

Quincannon nodded. "Where he'd just finished shooting McClellan and knocking me on the head."

Angry exclamations from the miners now, a trio of obscenities from Walrus Ben.

One of the men demanded of Quincannon, "What were *you* doing back at the cut?"

Briefly he explained the reason and told of his discovery of the tube mill and cache of gold dust. "Either Tremayne had a prearranged meeting there with McClellan, or he went to pick up the dust. He's the one who has been smuggling it out at regular intervals. A shift boss doesn't have to submit to routine inspections like the rest of you."

"That's right, he doesn't," Barnes muttered. "Be easy as pie for him."

"After knocking me senseless, he found the tube mill, sack of dust, and derringer in my pockets. If McClellan hadn't come along just then, the gun might well have been used on me. Tremayne used it on his cohort instead, after they carried me back into the cut. McClellan knew I was on to him, he was losing his nerve, and like as not he wanted no part of murder. It was the perfect opportunity for Tremayne to eliminate both threats at once, by shooting McClellan and framing me for the deed."

"How? How could he have done it? He was with us when the shot was fired . . ."

"No he wasn't. The killing was done several minutes earlier, before he sought you out. What you heard was what he brought you along to hear—the explosion of a blasting cap."

"By God! Now I think of it, the report did sound too loud for that of a derringer."

"Tremayne is a powder man," Quincannon said, "and I've heard miners say that a good blaster can blow a man's nose for him without mussing his hair. He carries those little copper detonators in his pocket; you've all seen him take one out now and then, I'll wager, just as I have. He also carries lengths of Bickford fuse. Simple enough to cut a piece of just the length needed to give him enough time to gather witnesses, then crimp the fuse into one of the detonators and light it."

Quincannon's words had had the desired effect on the group of miners. They had shifted position so that now they had closed ranks around the shift boss, their cap lamps shining on his seamed, sweat-slick face.

"He made the mistake," Quincannon went on, "of laying the fuse in such a way that a portion of it burned black along the side and sole of McClellan's left boot. I discovered that yesterday afternoon, and this morning I found the exploded cap in the abandoned stope. That's all the evidence needed for proof of his guilt."

Walrus Ben maintained a dark and sullen silence.

Quincannon did not need to draw the sixty-eight-cent Sears, Roebuck Defender in order to take Tremayne out of the mine and deliver him to O'Hearn. The miners not only made no effort to prevent it, but an apologetic Pat Barnes and one of the other timbermen accompanied them as guards. Walrus Ben, wisely, gave no resistance.

17

QUINCANNON

James O'Hearn was by turns shocked, incredulous, outraged. When Quincannon finished repeating the charges against Walrus Ben, the mine superintendent went to loom above the chair in which the shift boss sat stone-faced and spine-stiffened.

"Why, damn you, Tremayne?" he demanded. "After a dozen years as a loyal company man, *why*?"

Walrus Ben raised his beetle-browed head. He said with dull defiance, "Loyal company man! What did that get me, working down in the goddamn hole six days a week all those years?"

"It got you promoted to shift boss."

"Sure, for a few dollars more a month. It also got me weak lungs from the rock gas explosion down on eight-hundred five years ago. What the hell did I have to look forward to? Nothing but another couple of years until I couldn't do the job anymore and a disabled old age on the dole."

"So that's why you turned traitor."

"Traitor, hell. I don't owe you or Monarch anything more than a day's work for a day's pay, and that's what I gave you. Even after the high-grading started, you got that from me same as always."

"I also got a dead assistant foreman from you. Explain that away."

Tremayne sat stone-faced again.

"Traitor I can understand," O'Hearn said, "but not cold-blooded murderer. First McClellan, then the attempt on Quincannon in the chute this morning—"

"Wasn't my idea."

"Nobody else was around when you shot McClellan."

"I didn't mean McClellan," the shift boss said sullenly. "That was an accident. Frank lost his head when he saw the ore-crushing hideout had been found. I had the derringer in my hand, he tried to grab it, and it went off. Only choice I had then was to put the blame on Quinn, or whatever his name is. I couldn't shoot him, too, in cold blood. I'm not made that way, no matter what you think."

"No? What about the chute attempt?"

"Simcox's stupid notion, not mine. I had nothing to do with it."

"Whose stupid notion was the high-grading? Yours?"

"No."

"Who, then? Simcox? McClellan?"

"Hah. Neither of them had the brains or the guts to come up with the plan, much less set it all up."

Quincannon said, "Yost. He's the ringleader."

Walrus Ben didn't deny it. He blew out a heavy, coughing breath, as if expelling the last of his defiance. You could see in his eyes what took its place: the fatalism that sooner or later befell most criminals facing long prison terms or the hangman's noose. Questions would produce answers more readily now. "That's right," he said in flattened tones, "Yost. Smart bastard, whip-smart. Not the first time he put together a deal like this."

"How did you get mixed up with him?"

"Simcox. Joe knew him from one of those other deals."

"Yost isn't his right name. What is?"

"Only name I know him by."

"He's not a union representative. What does he do besides put together high-grading schemes?"

"He never said and I never asked." Tremayne's lips twisted in a humorless half grin. "Simcox probably knew, but he can't tell you now."

"Where did Yost go when he left here yesterday?"

Shrug.

"How much dust was he carrying with him?"

"Plenty. The biggest load so far. He had the rest of us working hard to mill as much as we could."

O'Hearn said, "And then you picked up the stashed dust, smuggled it out, and turned it all over to him."

"That was the arrangement."

"You hold out on him, did you?"

"No. Nobody did."

"You're wrong about that," Quincannon said. "McClellan managed to carry out some he kept for himself."

"The hell he did."

"At least two troy ounces, probably more."

"How do you know that?"

"How I know is no concern of yours. What is Yost planning to do with the load he carried off yesterday?"

"Same as before. Sell it for cash and pay off the rest of us in easier-to-spend greenbacks."

That confirmed Quincannon's theory. It also explained why Yost had made two short visits and the recent long one to Patch Creek—to collect the loot from Walrus Ben and to make sure the operation was running smoothly. "But you don't know where he does that kind of business?"

Headshake.

"Where did you first meet him? Not in Patch Creek?"

"No. Marysville."

"Is Marysville his home base?"

"Didn't seem so to me. Just a handy meeting place."

"Handy for him, too?"

Shrug.

Home-based in Sacramento, mayhap, Quincannon speculated. Or somewhere near the capital that allowed for a short train ride to Marysville. "Where in Marysville did the meeting take place?" he asked.

"Some tavern by the Yuba River," Tremayne said, "I don't remember the name. Simcox arranged it. Me and the others rode the stage down there on a Sunday."

"How long ago was that?"

"Four months. Early June. We started high-grading in July—took us a month to get everything set up."

O'Hearn asked, "How many others besides you, McClellan, and Simcox?"

"Three—one on the night shift, two on the graveyard," Walrus Ben said, and named them. None of the names was familiar to Quincannon.

O'Hearn had more questions: How many other ore-crushing hideouts were there and where were they located? How much had Walrus Ben and the others been paid so far? The answer to the first was three: one on eleven-hundred and two on twelve-hundred, all in abandoned crosscuts and stopes. The answer to the second increased the superintendent's ire. Some two thousand dollars had lined the pockets of each of the six conspirators, with the promise of another fifteen hundred or so to come. Yost would have kept a hefty cut of the profits for himself, at least 25 percent of the total take and probably more. All of which put the estimated value of the stolen gold in the neighborhood of $40,000—a substantial loss to Hoxley and Associates if most of the amount was not recovered.

The interrogation ended with the arrival of Sheriff Micah Calder, summoned by a messenger sent by O'Hearn. Calder looked and acted even more befuddled than usual, as if he was having difficulty comprehending that the Monarch Mine had been victimized by a high-grading gang led by the bogus Jedediah Yost, that it was Walrus Ben Tremayne who had shot and killed Frank McClellan, and that Quincannon was not only innocent of any wrongdoing but a San Francisco detective hired by Everett Hoxley. He kept shaking his head and passing such doltish remarks as "If that don't beat all" and "I be hornswoggled." He departed finally with the shift boss in handcuffs and instructions from O'Hearn to locate and arrest the three miners Tremayne had named.

When they were gone, O'Hearn sank heavily into his desk

chair and lighted a green-flecked cheroot. The fragrance of tobacco made Quincannon briefly long for his pipe and a bowl of Navy Cut.

"A damned sorry state of affairs, Quincannon. And still a long way from being finished. What do you intend to do about Yost and the gold dust he carted away yesterday?"

"Find him, and either the load of dust or its cash equivalent if he's had time for a quick sale."

"How? Ben wasn't lying about not knowing Yost's real name or where to find him."

"No," Quincannon agreed, "he wasn't lying."

"Well, then?"

"We'll start with a search of Simcox's belongings. Then Tremayne's, to make sure he was telling the truth; McClellan's again, if only to recover his stash of dust; and the trio of other conspirators. And we'll question those three as soon as they're in custody."

"And if none of that gives us a lead?"

"Then I'll commence a canvass of banks and private companies that buy large amounts of gold."

O'Hearn puffed hard on his cheroot, said through a mist of smoke, "That's assuming he's selling it on the legitimate market, not to some crooked underground outfit."

"He would do that only if he could get full dollar value for the gold, a highly unlikely prospect on the black market. My guess is that he has an arrangement with a quasi-legitimate firm that asks no questions about the source of the gold."

"If that's the case, he could be selling it to them as Yost, without giving his genuine address."

"Possibly, although even a quasi-legitimate institution requires valid identification for its transaction records."

"All right, but such a firm could be anywhere," O'Hearn argued. "It'll take weeks to canvass all the possible places."

"Not nearly that long, with my agency's resources."

"Suppose the right one can't be found. What then?"

Quincannon hedged by saying, "There are other methods of tracking down a fugitive."

"Such as?"

"None that need be shared. A detective of my caliber has certain trade secrets he reveals to no one."

The sound O'Hearn made was half growl, half snort. "Swatting yourself on the back again. Bah!"

"And with just cause. I exposed the high-graders and put an end to their game as promised, did I not? And in only ten days. So you needn't worry, Mr. O'Hearn. Yost won't get away with his ill-gotten gains."

"I'll stop worrying and admit you're as slick as you think you are when he's behind bars and restitution has been made. And it had better be soon."

Quincannon said, "Oh, it will be," with more conviction than he felt.

18

SABINA

Elmer J. Goodlove was waiting for her when she arrived at the Purifoy cottage on Monday afternoon. She was ten minutes early for their one o'clock appointment; Goodlove must have come quite a bit earlier than that, no doubt to make sure Vernon Purifoy was away at his job and the cottage empty, for he had already let himself inside. He popped out through the front door like a cuckoo bird out of a clock as she started up the cinder path. He wore his fat smile and an air of smug satisfaction. Bold as brass, Elizabeth Petrie had said he was. Indeed. As brazen a confidence trickster as Sabina had ever encountered.

"A very good day to you, Mrs. Fredericks," he said when she joined him at the top of the staircase. "I have excellent news. Excellent."

"So I surmised from your sudden appearance."

"I took the liberty of entering and having a brief look around. You don't mind, I trust?" His voice was as bubbly as champagne.

"The owner refused to sell at first, but I finally managed to convince him. Not an easy task, but Elmer Goodlove is never discouraged when acting on behalf of a determined client. No, never."

"For what price did he settle?"

"Ah, that was the sticking point, the price. We haggled for quite some time, but he wouldn't budge until I took it upon myself to make a final offer, one I felt he couldn't possibly refuse. And I was right—he didn't."

"A final offer of how much?"

The fat smile did not waver in the slightest. "A bit more than your expressed maximum, I'm afraid. Just a bit. But if you should object—"

"How much, Mr. Goodlove?"

"Three thousand five hundred. I sincerely hope I did not overstep in offering that much, but he really gave me no alternative."

Sabina was not in the least surprised. She said truthfully, "I detest a gouger. Who is he?"

"His name is, ah, Smith. Adam Smith. A bachelor of no consequence, a manufacturing company clerk, but stubborn and, yes, greedy." A pot calling a nonexistent kettle black, Sabina thought sardonically. "Is the price satisfactory, Mrs. Fredericks?"

"I will give you my answer after I've seen the interior."

"Of course. By all means. Shall we step inside?"

The front door opened into a narrow parlor. Goodlove shut the door quickly after they entered; Sabina sensed that he was relieved to be back inside, out of public view, even though there had been no one in the vicinity to observe their brief conversation.

You could tell quite a lot about a person by his home environment. Vernon Purifoy's parlor verified her perception of him.

The furnishings were few, old, and obviously inherited; no priggish martinet in his right mind would have picked out and bought the plum-colored velour sofa, for instance. The room was fussily neat, nothing at all out of place, but not so fussily clean. Speckles of dust marked the furniture, the fireplace mantel, the somewhat threadbare carpet. Gretchen Kantor's statement that he lived frugally was accurate.

One extended look around the parlor was sufficient, but she took a slow turn through it on the pretense of examining walls, ceiling, the bricks in the tiny fireplace. "Satisfactory thus far," she said to Goodlove. "Please wait here while I inspect the other rooms."

"Wait here? But . . ."

"I do not wish to be watched over or hurried. You have no objection, I trust?"

The only one Goodlove was likely to have concerned the length of time they remained in the cottage, but she had counted on greed outweighing caution, and so it did. "No objection, no indeed," he said. He took his fat body and fat smile to the velour sofa. "I'll just wait right here."

The remaining three rooms, not counting a closet-sized bathroom, were a small kitchen and two adjoining bedrooms. The first Sabina looked into contained a four-poster bed, a dresser, and a wardrobe, all of it as old and doubtless inherited as the parlor furniture. It was the second, converted into a spartan study, that contained the desk Miss Kantor had referred to—a well-used, factory-built Montgomery Ward rolltop.

Sabina shut the door quietly behind her, stood looking at the desk. None of the drawers on either side of the kneehole was locked; a glance through the contents of each revealed nothing of value or interest. The rolltop was locked down in place, but the lock appeared to be flimsy; an upward tug affirmed that the bolt was loose in its frame.

She hesitated, but only for a few moments. She had gone this far; she might as well go all the way.

John was an expert at picking locks; he often carried a set of burglar's picks and had no qualms about using them for illegal entry when he deemed it necessary. Normally she viewed the practice with a jaundiced eye, and she had never indulged in it herself, but as the saying went, there was a first time for everything. He had demonstrated his prowess to her on more than one occasion, so she knew the rudiments. And she did not need a set of picks for this particular task. Her Charles Horner hatpin, with its thin, needle-sharp point, would no doubt suffice.

It did, and after only a few series of jiggles and wiggles. She replaced the hatpin and slid the rolltop up as noiselessly as she could. The interior was in apple-pie order. Cubbyholes containing plain envelopes and notepaper, receipts for various services, Bank of California checking account receipts for small deposits and withdrawals. One of two drawers was filled with pencils, pens, erasers, postage stamps, a jar of India ink. The second, a keyhole drawer, was locked.

Charles Horner made short work of opening it. Inside were two manila envelopes with looped-string clasps. And inside the first envelope was a sheaf of bank draft deposit receipts bound with a rubber band. Not from the Bank of California or any other local institution, but from the Citizens Bank of New Orleans. Sabina shuffled through them. All were made out to the Jackson Investment Company of San Francisco, S. Jackson, president, each for monthly deposits over the past two years in amounts ranging from $250 to $1,000—an aggregate, at a quick estimate, of nearly $20,000.

Where had Purifoy, with his frugal ways and doubtless modest accountant's salary, come into possession of such a sum of money? And why was he putting it into a bank in far-off New Orleans under the name S. Jackson?

The contents of the second envelope supplied the answers. More receipts, and a small ledger book neatly filled with names, dates, and dollar figures. The figures correlated exactly to those deposited to the Jackson Investment Company, the origins of which were monthly payments by the Hollowell Manufacturing Company to Western Pacific Supply and Cosgrove Ironworks. The receipts showed regular withdrawals of those monthly payments from the accounts of the two firms, each at a different bank, by their owners and proprietors, Aurelius D. Jones and George Cosgrove. All of which added up to one indisputable fact.

Vernon Purifoy was an embezzler.

And so meticulous in his accountant's ways, so foolishly cocksure, that he had kept a complete written record of his thefts, as well as receipts that revealed his planned destination once he was ready to quit his job, sell or abandon this cottage, and head to New Orleans.

Well, Sabina? Now that you know Mr. Purifoy's secret, what are you going to do about it?

Putting the envelopes back where she'd found them was out of the question. She and Charles Horner might not be able to relock both the drawer and the rolltop, and even if she tried she might not have enough time; Goodlove might grow tired of waiting and come looking for her. And once Purifoy found that the desk had been breached, it could spook him enough to destroy the evidence and immediately take himself on the lammas. The same was true if he found the envelopes missing, but the evidence would be intact and secure.

Her bag was just large enough to accommodate both envelopes. She tucked them inside, then slid the rolltop down and left the room.

Goodlove bounced to his feet when she entered the parlor. "All finished with your inspection, Mrs. Fredericks?" he said, baring his teeth again. "You found everything satisfactory?"

"Quite satisfactory, yes."

"Excellent. Then you're amenable to paying Mr. Smith's asking price?"

"I am. Though I must say the amount does not please me."

"Of course, of course. Shall we leave, then?"

He managed to steer her to the door without seeming to do so, then peered out before allowing her to precede him. A conveyance passed on the street as they stepped out and descended the staircase, but none of the occupants paid any attention to them. Goodlove's step grew jaunty once they exited the property, a measure of his relief that the illegal trespass had been accomplished without incident.

He said then, "I have taken the liberty of drawing up an agreement which Mr. Smith has already signed. Shall we proceed to my office and complete the transaction? I have a buggy parked just down the block—"

"Not today, no. I am not prepared to make payment just yet. Three thousand five hundred dollars is more than I have in my personal account at present."

"A post-dated check would be acceptable."

"I prefer that funds be in the account before writing a check. I will make the necessary arrangements with my husband and our bank."

"Ah, if you are able to do that today, perhaps we could meet later—"

Sabina said, sharpening her autocratic tone, "You needn't be so eager, Mr. Goodlove. One would think you lack trust in my wherewithal to consummate the transaction."

"Oh, no, dear lady, nothing of the sort. I merely assumed you would wish to do so immediately. At your convenience, by all means."

"Tomorrow, then. No, Wednesday would be better—my husband is quite busy and an extra day might be needed to secure the funds. One o'clock Wednesday at your office, shall we say?"

Goodlove knew better than to argue; he said one o'clock Wednesday would be perfectly acceptable. They had reached the buggy, an equipage as nondescript as the swindler and his office, and he offered her a ride to wherever she wished to go. She declined. She had spent as much time with him as she could stomach.

The last thing he said to her was, "Goodbye for now, Mrs. Fredericks. It has been a great pleasure doing business with you."

No, you tubby toad, Sabina thought as the buggy rattled away, the pleasure is entirely mine.

19

SABINA

The Hall of Justice, to which she went directly after leaving Potrero Hill, stood opposite Portsmouth Square on Kearney between Washington and Merchant streets—a gloomy pile that was scheduled for an overdue reconstruction. The last time she had come here was several months ago, on a rather brazen mission to the city morgue in the company of Charles Percival Fairchild the Third, the canny crackbrain who fancied himself to be the famous British detective Sherlock Holmes. That had been her last encounter with Charles the Third, who at the time had been unjustly accused of the murder of his Chicago cousin, and who had left the city for parts unknown shortly after she played a significant role in exonerating him. As annoying and intrusive as he'd been on several occasions, she retained a soft spot for him—it was he who had gifted her with her cat Eve, among other courtesies—and wished him well wherever he'd gone and whatever he was up to.

Women other than police matrons and Barbary Coast streetwalkers being taken to the basement city prison were a rarity at the Hall of Justice, especially young, attractive, stylishly dressed women. Sabina was the recipient of several admiring glances and a smattering of leers from uniformed officers and other men when she entered, while she was requesting an audience with Lieutenant Asa Brinkman of the Fraud Division, and as she was being escorted to his office on the second floor. All of which unwanted flattery she ignored.

Brinkman, despite his fifty-some years and position of command, was not averse to giving her a similarly appreciative once-over. His smile turned upside down, however, when she identified herself.

"The notorious lady detective," he said.

"Notorious?"

"You and your partner both. Numerous instances of interference in police matters—the homicide at the Baldwin Hotel and that Chinatown body-snatching sensation, among others."

"Cases we were drawn into unwillingly. And which, I might point out, we had a strong hand in resolving."

"By devious means, according to some reports."

Meaning newspaper reports, Sabina thought, specifically Homer Keeps's columns in the muckraking *Evening Bulletin*. That nasty little troll took perverse delight in denigrating the good works done by Carpenter and Quincannon, Professional Detective Services. His innuendos as to their honesty and integrity always stopped just short of libel; otherwise he would have faced a defamation suit. Thus far Keeps's scurrilous attacks were viewed by most for what they were—pure claptrap—and had done no harm to their business.

"Untrue, I assure you," she said. "Ours is a reputable agency, always ready and willing to cooperate with the police. Which is why I've come to see you today."

Brinkman remained skeptical. He was gray-haired and blue-jowled, his nose and cheeks spider-webbed with broken capillaries that attested to a chronic overindulgence in alcoholic beverages. A fondness for rich food was evidently another of his vices; his broad torso and thick neck strained the buttons on his uniform tunic.

"I have information I think you'll find pleasing, Lieutenant. It concerns a real estate swindler who operated in the city eight years ago, under the name Harold Newcastle."

"Newcastle?" The results of a brief memory search altered Brinkman's expression. "How did you come across that piece of ancient history?"

"It's no longer ancient history," Sabina said. "He has come back and is running the same game as before."

"The devil he has! He wouldn't dare! You must be mistaken."

"A tubby little man with white hair and a cheerful smile. Is that the description you had of Harold Newcastle?"

"Yes, but I still can't believe—"

"Some confidence men are fearless risk-takers, as you well know. Especially when they have succeeded in flaunting the law over a long span of time."

"True enough," Brinkman admitted. "He's running the same swindle here in the city, you're sure of that?"

"Exactly the same. Selling vacant lots and homes he doesn't own for whatever down payments his victims are willing to part with."

"By Christ, it does sound like the same man. He isn't still calling himself Harold Newcastle?"

"No. Elmer J. Goodlove. Goodlove Real Estate, 1006 Guerrero Street. Surely all the proof necessary for his arrest and eventual conviction is to be found there."

Brinkman repeated the name and address, then went to his desk and wrote them down. When he came back to face Sabina, he said, "I still want to know how you came by this information."

Time for another white lie. "It was revealed during the course of an investigation that has nothing to do with Goodlove," she said. "Or with real estate, except indirectly. An ancillary discovery, as it were."

"What does your investigation have to do with?"

"I am not at liberty to divulge that. Suffice it to say that it is extensive and completely legal, for a client who shuns publicity and demands discretion." She paused for effect. "Nabbing an elusive swindler is the important thing, isn't it, Lieutenant?"

"As long as what you've told me is the truth."

"It is. And I ask no credit for it."

"No? I suppose you brought this to my attention out of civic duty."

"Exactly. As I said before, my partner and I believe in cooperating with the police." Sabina favored him with a conspiratorial smile. "You could say in your report that you received an anonymous tip."

"So I could." And so he would, if she was any judge of character. A resolute gleam shone in his eyes now. Plainly he was thinking that not having to share credit for closing an old and nettlesome case would be a large feather in his cap.

He said, "Very well, Mrs. Carpenter, I'll take you at your word. Is there anything more you have to tell me before you depart?"

Sabina took a tighter grip on her well-stuffed handbag. "No," she said. "Nothing more."

At Carpenter and Quincannon, Professional Detective Services, she consulted the office set of various city business directories. As she'd suspected, Western Pacific Supply and Cosgrove Ironworks were nonexistent companies created by Vernon Purifoy. Their alleged respective owners, Aurelius D. Jones and George Cosgrove, were established aliases, their invoices for goods supplied to and paid for by the Hollowell Manufacturing Company bogus. It had been simple enough for Purifoy, masquerading as Jones and Cosgrove, to regularly withdraw funds from the two dummy accounts and to then arrange for the drafts to be sent to the New Orleans bank. A clever and profitable embezzlement scheme that had gone undetected because Purifoy, as chief accountant, authorized payments of all monthly invoices submitted by Hollowell suppliers and sub-contractors. Obviously he was considered a trusted employee and his books had never been audited.

She had already decided what she must do. The proper course of action was to personally deliver the two envelopes to the Hollowells, *per et fils*, but that was out of the question for the same reason she had not informed the police of Purifoy's crime: it would mean admitting that she had come into possession of the evidence by means of illegal trespass and theft from a locked desk. Nor could she attempt to swear the Hollowells to secrecy; if they refused, she would be subject to an additional criminal complaint. Not only would her freedom be in jeopardy, but so would the agency's good name and her future with John.

But neither, in all good conscience, could she allow Vernon Purifoy to continue misappropriating funds from his employers. The only way she could see to prevent that, and at the same time protect herself, meant once more compromising her professional ethics. So be it, then. As John was fond of saying, the end did sometimes justify the means.

From the office storeroom she fetched a small carton, a roll of wrapping paper, and a ball of stout twine. Then, on a sheet of plain paper, she wrote in a slanted backhand: **Vernon Purifoy is an embezzler. Here is proof.** She put the manila envelopes into the carton, wrapped it several times around, and secured it with the twine. In the same backhand she penned a gummed label to both Lucas J. and Norman A. Hollowell at the Stevenson Street address, and marked it **PERSONAL AND PRIVATE** in large letters.

It was past five o'clock by the time she finished, too late to have the package delivered to Hollowell Manufacturing today. She locked it in the office safe for protection overnight. First thing tomorrow she would arrange delivery by messenger, utilizing a trustworthy service that guaranteed the sender's anonymity.

What was not guaranteed was that she would remain anonymous. It was possible that either Purifoy or Gretchen Kantor would connect her with his unmasking and so inform the authorities. It was also possible, if less likely, that Elmer Goodlove would make a similar connection to his sudden exposure and arrest and tell of their illegal trespass into Purifoy's cottage. If either or both should happen, she would have to confess and explain that she had acted with the best of intentions. The only alternative, weaving another web of white lies in the hope they would be believed, was out of the question.

What a muddle these two intertwined cases had turned into. She had brought about the downfall of two felons in the span of two days, an accomplishment that under normal circumstances would have been a source of pride. Instead she faced the possibility that her rash actions would result in a downfall of her own.

And all because she had allowed herself to act on not just one but a series of whims.

REAL ESTATE SWINDLER ARRESTED

The headline topped a page 1 news story in Tuesday's edition of the *Morning Call*, a copy of which Sabina picked up at the newsstand operated by the "blind" vendor and underworld informant known as Slewfoot. She read the story avidly. Lieutenant Brinkman had wasted no time in making the pinch and obtaining a full confession, and if Harold Newcastle alias Elmer J. Goodlove had said anything about Mrs. Jonathan Fredericks, there was no mention of it. Nor were any of his actual victims mentioned by name. The story focused on the nature of his crimes and his audacity in operating a swindle identical to the one he had perpetrated in the city in 1889. It also applauded the swift action taken by the head of the Fraud Division after receipt of an anonymous tip.

Sabina was both satisfied and relieved, her conscience now clear on at least this case. The doing of her "civic duty" had been rewarded in more ways than one.

Not long after the private messenger service picked up the package on Tuesday morning, a Western Union messenger brought her another wire. Again it was from Henry Flannery, this one a report that pleased her as much as the arrest of Newcastle/Goodlove.

Bartholomew Morgan had in fact returned to the state capital after being forced out of Downieville in 1887, four years later if not immediately. B. Morgan had been the proprietor of Delta Metallurgical Works in West Sacramento since 1891. And there could be no doubt that he was also Jedediah Yost, for he fit exactly the supplied physical description.

Now she had another decision to make. And she made it immediately, without a second thought.

20

QUINCANNON

He bid a none-too-fond farewell to the Monarch Mine and Patch Creek on Tuesday morning. A mixture of frustration and steadfast determination rode with him on the stage to Marysville. The various searches of Joe Simcox's living quarters and belongings and those of the other high-graders had not turned up the slightest lead to the whereabouts of the elusive Jedediah Yost. Interrogations of the three night-shift and graveyard-shift conspirators proved equally futile.

Quincannon's frustration increased in Marysville, for the train to Sacramento was delayed nearly two hours by some sort of problem on the right-of-way. He used part of the waiting time to compose and send a coded telegram to Sabina, informing her that he was alive and well and his undercover work at the Monarch Mine had been successfully completed. Naturally, he made no mention of such specifics as his arrest and overnight incarceration for the murder of Frank McClellan, or his narrow escape from the mine chute; those vexing matters were better discussed in person, if at all. About Jedediah Yost he wrote nothing, stating only that it was necessary he spend a day or two in Sacramento before returning to San Francisco and would be lodging at the Golden Eagle Hotel.

Most of the day was gone when the train finally deposited him at the main railroad station—too late to begin his inquiries into Yost's means of disposal of the stolen gold. Just as well, for the one good suit he'd brought with him, stored the past ten days in his war bag, was sorely in need of brushing and pressing, and he was sorely in need of a bath, a decent meal, and a night's sleep in a comfortable bed.

The Golden Eagle was his usual choice of hostelries on his infrequent visits to Sacramento. Its proximity to the Capitol Building made it a gathering spot for local and national politicians and the occasional residence of Republican governors and their families; Quincannon liked it anyway. It was, as its advertisements claimed, a "strictly first-class" establishment, offering accommodations and a restaurant bill of fare the near equal of those in the Palace and Baldwin hotels in San Francisco. Expensive, of course, which went against his thrifty Scot's nature, but he would include the cost on the Hoxley and Associates expense account for reimbursement. Besides, he was entitled to pamper himself when circumstances warranted it.

The Golden Eagle provided free transportation by carriage from the railroad depot and steamboat landings. Quincannon availed himself of the service and was delivered more or less promptly to the hotel. The three-story, two-hundred-room edifice on the corner of 7th and K streets had been built in 1863 on land raised by the construction of reinforced brick walls filled with dirt, the raising having been necessary after floodwaters from the American and Sacramento rivers inundated the downtown area in the winter of 1861. The first floors of many buildings had become basements as a result, with what had previously been sidewalks now at the basement level.

The amount of pedestrian, equipage, and light-rail traffic appeared to have increased since Quincannon's last visit. Once a settlement founded when gold was discovered at Sutter's Mill in '48, Sacramento had grown over the past half century and was now bordering on a metropolis. The city had prospered first as the hub of supplies freighted to the gold fields in the Mother Lode and across the mountains to the silver boomtown of Virginia City, then as an agricultural shipping point. Its location at the confluence of the two rivers allowed it to control commerce on both, and the levying of tariffs on goods transported by competing railroads during and after the Civil War increased its economic success. A boast had been made that there were as many millionaires among its citizenry as resided in San Francisco. True or not, Quincannon was of the opinion that it had just as many robber barons, not a few of whom occupied seats in the state legislature.

His rumpled suit and war bag were given a disdainful glance by the Golden Eagle's door porter. Quincannon repaid him with a long and equally disdainful glower, took a firmer grip on the bag, and toted it across the ornately appointed lobby. The clerk at the registration desk, a middle-aged fellow with a starched face to match his starched collar, had no better manners than the porter, but they improved somewhat when Quincannon stated that he had been a guest of the hotel on several previous occasions. Rooms were always kept available on short notice to repeat customers.

"Your name, sir?"

"John Frederick Quincannon. Of Carpenter and Quincannon, Professional Detective Services, San Francisco."

The clerk cocked his head to one side, birdlike. "We didn't expect you, Mr. Quincannon. Naturally you will require a second room."

"Second room?"

"Unless of course you are married."

"Married? Why should that matter to you?"

"Sir," the clerk said a bit stiffly, "we are a conservative establishment. We do not allow ladies and gentlemen to occupy the same room without benefit of clergy."

Quincannon looked at him askance. "What the devil are you talking about?"

"The wire we received specifically requested a single room reservation."

"Wire from whom?"

"Presumably your, ah, business associate, Mrs. Sabina Carpenter."

Sabina! Quincannon managed not to gawp his astonishment. "When did you receive the wire?"

"This morning."

"What time this morning?"

"I don't recall the exact time, sir."

"But it was before noon?"

"Yes, it was. Shortly after ten o'clock."

"For when and how long was the accommodation requested?"

"For tonight and possibly tomorrow night. You were not aware that Mrs. Carpenter would be joining you, sir?"

"Of course I was," Quincannon lied. "My surprise is due to her failure to request a reservation for me as well. She must have assumed I had done so myself. I have been away on business for some time and we planned to meet here before I left."

"I see. You will require a room of your own, then?"

"Certainly. Mrs. Carpenter is a widow and I am unmarried. Our relationship is strictly professional."

The clerk said he had no doubt of that, a probable lie of his own.

"Mrs. Carpenter hasn't checked in yet, I presume?"

"No, sir. Her wire stated that she expected to arrive early evening. Would you care to leave a message for her?"

"That won't be necessary."

Quincannon forbore asking if a room had been assigned to Mrs. Carpenter, and if so, one for himself nearby. It would only have made the clerk more doubtful. He signed the register and was given a room with a private bath on the second floor.

A uniformed bellhop and an elevator conducted him upstairs. In the room, small but well appointed, he asked the bellhop for valet service and handed him a nickel—an indication of how distracted he was by the news of Sabina's imminent arrival. Usually he took a dim view of the practice of tipping.

Coincidences were not uncommon in detective work, but this one was somewhat staggering and not a little perplexing. She couldn't possibly have known he would be in Sacramento today; his wire from Marysville hadn't been sent until a few minutes past noon. She had to be making the trip for some purpose of her own, and had chosen the Golden Eagle because she knew of his preference for the establishment. A stopover on her way to Patch Creek, where she thought him to be, to bring him vital information of some sort? Possibly, but then why had her wire to the hotel stated that she might be staying more than one night?

Well, there was no sense in tying his brain in knots attempting to answer the temporarily unanswerable. He would have a full account when Sabina arrived.

He shed his suit and waistcoat, and when the valet came knocking, turned the articles over to him for immediate brushing and pressing. Then he drew a bath in the clawfoot tub, and sat for the better part of an hour soaking his sore muscles and washing away the last of ten days of Monarch-induced grit, grime, and sweat. He was finishing a trim of his whiskers when the valet returned. Dressed in his last clean shirt and freshened clothing, he decided, on a mirror inspection, that he was presentable enough to meet his betrothed. The prospect excited him, not because of whatever reason Sabina had for coming here, but because he would be with her again much sooner than anticipated.

He considered spit-polishing his shoes, decided against it, and rode the elevator down to the lobby. At a shoeshine stand in the hotel barbershop he paid for an expert buffing and polishing and tipped the Negro lad a nickel. This time it was because contemplation of the fee and large bonus he would receive from Everett Hoxley had put him in an expansive mood. Why not share the wealth with those less fortunate?

It was after five o'clock when he reentered the lobby. His stomach was making ominous grumbling noises—his only provender for the day had been a tasteless sandwich in Marysville—but dining alone tonight had no appeal. Besides, he did not want to be in the midst of a meal when Sabina arrived.

He bought the most recent edition of the *Sacramento Bee*, found a comfortable leather chair within view of the registration desk, and settled down to wait.

21

SABINA

Sabina thought her eyes must be playing tricks on her.

It had been a long, tiresome day. The day coach on the train from Oakland had been crowded and stuffy, her seatmate a fat man who smelled of cheap cigars and bay rum. Three hours in his proximity plus a lack of food had given her a throbbing headache. The edges of her vision were slightly blurry, and the Golden Eagle's electric-lighted chandeliers were bright enough to cause her to squint as she started across the crowded lobby, a bellhop carrying her carpetbag two steps behind. The bearded, neatly dressed man who rose from one of the chairs and came toward her made only a vague impression at first, then as he drew closer she saw that he bore a remarkable resemblance to John. She blinked, passed a hand over her eyes. It couldn't *be* John—

But it was.

She came to such an abrupt standstill, confusion mingling

with surprise, that the porter nearly stumbled into her. He retreated as a smiling John reached her and took her arm. "Hello, my dear," he said. "Fancy us meeting like this so far from home."

"John! What are you doing *here*?"

"What are *you* doing here?"

She felt a trifle faint, a rarity for her under any circumstances. She steadied herself by leaning against his arm. The bellhop was staring at them; so were two passersby in silk hats and evening clothes. She said sotto voce, "We can't have a discussion standing here among all these people."

"No, we can't."

He guided her to the registration desk, stood by while she signed the register. Then he drew her aside, out of earshot of the clerk and other guests hovering near the desk.

"Have you eaten?" he asked.

"No. And I'm half starved."

"So am I. We can converse over dinner."

"I need to freshen up first."

He nodded. "I'll wait for you here. Don't be too long, my dear."

"I won't."

Sabina followed the bellhop up to her reserved room on the third floor. She washed her face, applied a small amount of rouge to her cheeks (her skin struck her as pale), brushed and repinned her hair, and exchanged her gray serge traveling dress and Langtry bonnet for the only semiformal outfit she'd brought with her: an ivory white shirtwaist with ruffles capping the shoulder, a pale green skirt that fitted closely over the hip and flared just above the knee, and a small black turban hat. The other outfit in her hastily packed bag was the least conservative in her wardrobe, bought for the infrequent occasions when circumstances required her to pose as a commoner. Now, fortunately, it seemed she would not have to wear it after all.

John had reserved a private table in the elegantly appointed dining room. A white-jacketed waiter set bills of fare in front of them, then took Sabina's order for a glass of cream sherry and John's for warm clam juice.

John placed her hand between both of his. "Two weeks is a long time for us to have been parted," he said. "I missed you, my dear."

"And I you. It's a relief to see you hale and hearty, John. No visible scars."

He started an involuntary reach for his missing earlobe, stopped himself halfway, and lowered his hand. He said with a mild leer, "Nor any hidden ones, as you'll soon see."

Sabina let that pass without comment. "Did you succeed in ferreting out the high-graders?"

"I did, and in less than half the time allotted by Everett Hoxley. There'll be no more organized gold thievery at the Monarch Mine. Two of the gang are dead—not by my hand, I hasten to add—and the rest in jail. All that is except one, the ringleader."

"Jedediah Yost?"

"None other."

"And he is the reason you're in Sacramento?"

"Yes. He slipped out of Patch Creek with a large amount of gold dust on Sunday, and I suspect he came here to dispose of it. He is no more a union representative than I am, and the

Yost cognomen is an alias. A sly, canny devil, whatever his real name."

"Bart Morgan," Sabina said.

His jaw dropped. He fluffed his whiskers, as he sometimes did when taken aback, before saying, "Bart Morgan? That is Yost's real name?"

"It is. Bartholomew Morgan."

"Are you certain?"

"Positive. He is an assayer and metallurgist by trade, with a highly disreputable past."

"An assayer. Of course! That explains his knowledge of gold mining and of where to sell the stolen gold at the best possible price. How did you find out about him?"

There was no sense in hiding or evading the truth. She'd done enough of that the past few days, far too much of it. "From Carson Montgomery. He was acquainted with Morgan briefly in Downieville ten years ago and recognized him from his description."

John said through a scowl, "So Morgan was one of the thieves Montgomery was mixed up with back then, eh?"

"No. Carson had no dealings with Morgan, knew him only by reputation."

"So he claimed to you. I thought you wanted nothing more to do with the man."

"I don't in the way you mean," Sabina said, "nor does he with me. I went to see him in his office as a last resort, when all my other efforts to find out Yost's true identity failed."

John made a grumbling noise in his throat, but if he intended a further challenge, the arrival of their drinks forestalled it. Sabina's empty stomach had set up a grumbling of its own; if she didn't eat soon, her lingering headache would worsen. She asked the waiter for a dinner recommendation, and was told that the brook trout almondine was quite good. She ordered that and creamed asparagus, and a bowl of clam chowder to start. John, who usually preferred to make his own dinner selections, said he would have the same without consulting the menu.

"Is what you found out about Morgan the reason you came to Sacramento?" he asked her when they were alone again.

"Part of the reason, yes. Carson remembered that Morgan's wife was from Sacramento and yearned to return, so it seemed possible that he might have moved here from Downieville."

"What were you planning to do? Travel to Patch Creek to pass the information on to me?"

"I thought you'd want to know as soon as possible, and there was no better way of informing you."

"How would you have informed me, thinking as you must have been that I was still working undercover as a miner?"

That had been a problem, as Sabina pointed out when Callie had tendered the notion of her going to Patch Creek. She had solved it in the cab she'd hired to take her to her flat to pack for the trip. She would pose as J. F. Quinn's sister bearing news of a family tragedy, a plausible means of getting a message to him that would not have jeopardized his mission. That had been the reason she'd packed the one dowdy outfit she owned, to disguise her breeding and physical attributes when she arrived in Patch Creek.

When she related the method to John, he said reprovingly,

"A gold camp is a perilous place for a respectable woman of any class. And you couldn't possibly look unattractive no matter how you're dressed."

"A roundabout compliment, but thank you."

He didn't pursue the issue, instead quaffed some of his warm clam juice. He had taken to the stuff after making his private temperance pledge seven years ago as a nonalcoholic substitute for whiskey. To each his own. Sabina had nothing against clams per se, or else she would not have ordered the chowder, but she found the warm juice unpalatable.

"You said Morgan's identity was part of the reason you came here," he said. "What is the other part?"

"I know where you can find him."

"You do? Confound it, why didn't you tell me that straightaway?"

"I would have if you hadn't castigated me."

"Faugh. Well? Where can I find him?"

"He owns and operates an assay shop, Delta Metallurgical Works, in West Sacramento."

"Did you find that out from Montgomery, too?"

"No. From Henry Flannery."

"Flannery? You brought him into it?"

"And why not? He is a very good investigator—it took him only a short time to locate Morgan."

"Good, yes, but his fees are too high."

"So are ours on occasion, when you have your way."

John dismissed that remark with a grunt. "The address of Delta Metallurgical Works?"

"Ninety-seven Poplar Avenue."

He sat in silence for a time, his jaw set, his gaze focused inward. She knew what he was thinking. "It would be folly to go out there alone tonight," she said. "Morgan may not live on the premises—Flannery's wire didn't say—and I don't suppose you're familiar with the area. Are you?"

"No."

"Then wait until morning and I'll go there with you."

He maintained the introspective pose a few seconds longer, then shook himself and said, "I'll wait until then, but you'll not go with me. Morgan is a dangerous man."

"I know. He reputedly killed a rival in Downieville. You mustn't go after him alone. Take Flannery with you."

"At his hourly rates?"

"John, for heaven's sake!"

". . . All right, I'll take Flannery if he's available."

Their clam chowder arrived. While they ate John launched into an account of his feats of deduction and derring-do in Patch Creek. No doubt some of it was embellished by his flair for the dramatic, and she had the feeling that he left out certain details and glossed over others that concerned personal perils he'd faced. Just as well. She had no desire to know what those perils were. All that mattered was that he had survived his time in the depths of the Monarch Mine unscathed.

He finished his oratory just before the waiter brought their entrees. He asked then what she had been up to during his absence besides consulting with Carson Montgomery (she had to admit she found his unwarranted jealousy both gratifying and amusing). Had there had been any new clients or prospects?

She would have relished telling him of her dual triumphs in

ending the criminal careers of a confidence man and an embezzler. In a sense both cases had a certain parallel to John's investigation. What, after all, were the cash Goodlove had bilked from his clients and the $20,000 Vernon Purifoy had misappropriated but forms of stolen gold?

But of course she didn't dare mention either. Mainly because John would have chastised her, and rightly so, for her impulsive and unprofessional behavior, but also because in neither of the two cases had Carpenter and Quincannon, Professional Detective Services, had a paying client or earned so much as one thin dime—a cardinal sin, to John's way of thinking. She said only that business had been very slow, which was true enough, and that she had been bored much of the time, which was also true.

Over dessert, an excellent crème brûlée, she steered the conversation to their nuptials and honeymoon plans. But she could tell that John's enthusiasm for both was tempered by unfinished business, and that his thoughts kept wandering to Bartholomew Morgan and tomorrow's hoped-for confrontation in West Sacramento. She couldn't fault him. The slate needed to be wiped clean before either of them could concentrate on their future.

The meal cured her headache, but it also made her sleepy. John didn't object when she refused coffee, saying she wanted to retire early. He escorted her to her room, and it was a measure of his preoccupation that he did not ask to be invited in. She would have issued a firm rebuke if he had; this was neither the time nor the place for another premarital dalliance. He merely gave her cheek a chaste peck, said he would call for her at seven-thirty for breakfast, and took his leave.

Lying in bed, she wondered if she ought to insist on joining

John and Henry Flannery tomorrow. The prospect of waiting here for his return was disconcerting. Besides, it was through her efforts that he was on the trail of Bart Morgan, and no matter how volatile the man might be, she had never shied away from danger. But would he permit it? He might, if she promised to keep out of harm's way.

No, he *would* accede, she thought just before sleep claimed her, because she would not take no for an answer . . .

22

QUINCANNON

Henry Flannery resembled an aging politician, a likeness he cultivated by dressing in expensively tailored business suits and gold-chain-draped waistcoats, smoking expensive Cuban cigars, and affecting a loquacious hail-fellow-well-met persona. He was stout, seemed soft and flabby but wasn't, and sported a shortened, bushy, imperial beard. His office on J Street was larger and more expensively furnished than that of Carpenter and Quincannon, Professional Detective Services, and was presided over by a comely red-haired secretary young enough to be his daughter—both of which facts induced envy and mild rancor in Quincannon. There was, however, no question of Flannery's competence, or of his regard for Quincannon's—hence their quid pro quo arrangement. Though that might not continue if Flannery didn't lower his blasted fees.

"One hundred dollars to locate Bartholomew Morgan? An outrageously inflated sum."

"Not at all," Flannery said cheerfully. "Two days' work at fifty dollars per is not only fair but represents a generous discount. My usual fee is sixty dollars per day."

"Bah. All you did was locate his business in West Sacramento. You didn't even find out whether or not he also resides there."

"I doubt that he does, given the location. And neither he nor a Mrs. B. Morgan is listed in the residential section of the City Directory."

"Yes, well, and now you want another hundred dollars to accompany me out there."

"Accompany *us*," Sabina said.

Quincannon kept his glower on Flannery. He was irked at himself for having given in to her insistence on joining this morning's mission; a possible confrontation with a thief and reputed murderer was no venue for a woman, even one as capable and fearless as Sabina. But he never could refuse her when her mind was made up.

He said, "Well, Flannery?"

"The fee includes use of my private equipage for transportation to and from West Sacramento and to the constabulary here if Morgan is in our custody. Also hazardous-duty pay."

"What do you mean, hazardous duty? I'll be the one to confront Morgan, not you."

"Then why do you want me along? To protect Mrs. Carpenter?"

"I do not need protecting," Sabina said. "I won't be in the way."

Quincannon said to Flannery, "In case it takes two of us to

subdue Morgan, not that I expect it will. But I won't pay you extra to do nothing more than stand by."

Flannery chewed on his unlit cigar, shrugged. "Very well, then. Eighty dollars if stand by is all I am required to do."

Eighty was still exorbitant, but further haggling was a waste of time. "I'll need the loan of a pistol. All I have with me is a twin-barrel derringer."

"Certainly. Any preference?"

"I don't suppose you have a Navy Colt?"

"No. Do you normally carry such an outmoded weapon?"

Quincannon bristled at that. "Outmoded? Not when it has been converted to fire .38-caliber rimfire cartridges. What large-caliber weapon can you supply?"

"A Colt Peacemaker, if that will do."

"It will. And don't tell me you intend to charge for the loan?"

"Not unless you fire it."

"Faugh! And if I should?"

"The fee would depend on the number of rounds fired and whether there is any damage to the weapon."

"Flannery, you're a blasted bloodsucker."

"Not at all. Merely an astute businessman."

"Yes? Well, so am I. Next time you ask something of us, you'll pay and pay dear for it."

Flannery smiled good-naturedly. "Quid pro quo," he said.

Flannery's private equipage was a newish four-wheel brougham, all black, including curtains and sidelamps, drawn by a blue dun—the kind of conveyance that could be driven anywhere, from high-toned neighborhoods to slums, without attracting undue attention. Quincannon and Sabina sat on comfortable tufted leather seats inside. He half expected a hired driver, but no, Flannery took the reins himself.

Quincannon felt the prod of envy again as they set off, though such a vehicle was an extravagance better suited to this flatland country than to hilly San Francisco, and more cheaply housed here as well. He and Sabina had discussed purchasing a carriage for their personal as well as professional use, which they could certainly afford, but he had not been able to justify the outlay of funds. Perhaps the time had come to take the plunge now that they were about to be man and wife, and hang the expense. The cost could be recouped by raising their agency rates to the level of Flannery's.

West Sacramento was one of three small communities on the opposite shore of the Sacramento River, the other two being Bryte and Broderick. During the Gold Rush, it had been a settlement stop for California Steam Navigation Company riverboats bearing travelers through then-treacherous marshlands to Sacramento and the gold fields. Nowadays it was primarily an agricultural and fishing center, though enough treasure seekers still mined the river's sloughs and byways to support small-scale assayers and outfitting merchants.

A short ferry ride transported them from Sacramento's public dock to West Sacramento's. Delta Metallurgical Works was situated a short distance from the waterfront landing, in a section mostly occupied by saloons, eateries, and transient lodging houses. As they clattered along Poplar Street, Flannery called down that their objective was coming up on the right. Quincannon unsnapped the side curtain, peered out.

The place was about the size of one of the miners' shacks in Patch Creek and no better constructed—a false-fronted, board-and-batten building flanked on one side by an ironmonger's shop and on the other by a lot containing the skeleton of a building under construction. Hardly a prosperous assay business, likely no more than a legitimate or semi-legitimate cloak for Bart Morgan's nefarious activities. A wooden sign tacked to the windowless wall next to the entrance gave its name in faded black letters. Atop the flat tar-paper roof, wisps of smoke curled out of a tin chimney stack into the morning overcast.

"Occupied," he said to Sabina, who was leaning sideways to look past him.

"By Morgan, I hope."

"We'll soon find out."

Flannery drove on a short distance, brought the carriage to a stop, and swung down. Quincannon adjusted the holster for the Colt Peacemaker that Flannery had supplied—the weapon was clean and well balanced, a reassuring weight on his hip—and opened the door. Before he stepped out, Sabina gripped his arm and urged him to caution.

"I am always cautious in these situations," he assured her.

"Not as much as you should be sometimes. Don't make me a widow before I become a bride."

"Not before, my dear, and not after."

There was little traffic on the street, few pedestrians on the sidewalks. A light, cold breeze carried the faint mingled odors of river mud and marsh growth. From somewhere downstream, a high-pitched whistle announced a steamboat's imminent arrival at the Sacramento dock.

When they reached the door to the assay building, Quincannon drew his coattail away from the Peacemaker and wrapped his fingers around the handle. He had not forgotten Morgan's lightning-fast draw in Patch Creek. Then he led the way inside, with Flannery close behind him.

Anticlimax.

The lone man in the cluttered room was not Bart Morgan.

He half turned when he heard the door open—a scrawny, vulpine individual who had lived some sixty years and had half a dozen strands of dark hair plastered to a liver-spotted scalp. He said, "Be with you in a minute, gents," and turned away to close the door to a glowing assay furnace.

Quincannon neither relaxed nor removed his hand from the butt of the Peacemaker. A long scan of the room, lighted by a pair of kerosene lamps, showed him a closed door at the rear. He moved ahead to a counter on which several ore samples were arranged, some of which had sat there untouched for so long they were coated with dust. Flannery hung back against the wall near the entrance.

The fox-faced man was now hovering over a plank bench strewn with sample sacks, molds, flux bins, tongs, cupels. He opened a glass case of balance scales, took one out, and set a chunk of ore on it. He was watching the balance needle quiver when Quincannon spoke sharply.

"Is the proprietor here?"

"Mr. Morgan? Nope," the man said without looking up.

"Anyone else besides you?"

"Nope. Just me, Floyd Tucker."

"You expect Morgan this morning?"

"Nope."

"That door at the rear. Where does it lead?"

"Storeroom."

Flannery, on his own initiative, went to open the door and look inside. He nodded once in confirmation before shutting it again and returning to his stance by the entrance.

Tucker's attention was still fixed on the balance scale. He made an adjustment that held the needle motionless, then squinted to read the gauge.

Quincannon said to him, "So Morgan doesn't live here."

"No, he sure don't."

"Where can I find him?"

"Can't say. Look, mister, I'll be with you directly—"

"You'll be with me right now," Quincannon said, and smacked the countertop with the flat of his hand. The ore samples jumped like hop toads and so did Tucker. He swung around, blinked, blinked again. More than one man had quailed at one of Quincannon's fearsome stares and Tucker was no exception.

"What's the idea?" he said. "You in a hurry?"

"That's right. In a hurry to find Morgan."

"Dunno where he is. I haven't seen him in two weeks."

Quincannon drew the Peacemaker, laid it on the counter. "You best not be lying to me."

The heat from the assay furnace had put a sheen of sweat on Tucker's face; the sight of the gun thickened it and broke it into runnels. He seemed to shrink another inch or two, and his

Adam's apple commenced a spasmodic bobbing in his scrawny throat.

"I ain't lying, mister. Honest. Two weeks since I seen Mr. Morgan, and he didn't tell me where he was headed or when he'd be back."

"How long have you worked for him?"

"Three years, off and on, since I moved up here from Modesto to live with my daughter after my wife passed away. Two, three days a week when he's busy elsewhere and there's enough work to do. Ain't been much, lately, and there'll be less come winter—"

Quincannon sliced a hand downward to cut off the babble of irrelevant words. "Where does Morgan live?"

"I don't know."

"You've worked for him three years and you don't know where he hangs his hat?"

"He never said and I never asked. None of my business." Tucker wiped his sweaty face with his shirtsleeve. His gaze kept shifting from Quincannon to the Peacemaker, and it made him anxious to please. "But wherever, it ain't likely around here."

"Why do you say that?"

"Man's got plenty of money, he don't live out here on the river unless he's a local bigwig. Mr. Morgan ain't one of those. He don't spend much time here at all."

"How do you know Morgan has plenty of money?"

"Must have—clothes he wears, fancy rig he drives. Sure didn't make it with this place. Must have another business somewhere else."

That he did. Gold thievery.

"Or maybe it's poker winnings," Tucker said. "I been told he plays a mean game of stud."

"Where does he play when he's in town?"

"Ace High Card Club, over on South Street. Always a poker game going on there."

"Anyone he plays with regularly?"

"I don't know, unless maybe Luke Jaeger."

"Who would Luke Jaeger be?"

"Owns the Ace High."

"All right," Quincannon said. He picked up the Peacemaker, hefted it in his hand. "My companion and I will be leaving now. Not that we were ever here."

Tucker said quickly, "Nobody's been here this morning, nobody at all."

"You won't forget that, will you?"

"No, sir, I sure won't."

Quincannon rearranged his expression to one less threatening, holstered the weapon, and went to the door. Flannery followed him out.

On the sidewalk Flannery said, "You handled the fellow rather well, Quincannon."

"Did you think I wouldn't? Or that you could have done better?"

"Now, don't be crusty. We're lodge brothers, after all."

"Bah."

Sabina had exited the brougham and was pacing along beside it. She said as they came up, "So Morgan wasn't there."

Quincannon wagged his head. "Nor will he be, evidently."

"Did you learn where to find him?"

"No, confound it. Not yet."

Flannery climbed up into the driver's seat, waited until his passengers were seated inside before saying to Quincannon, "Ace High Card Club?"

"Quick as you can get us there."

23

QUINCANNON

The Ace High Card Club occupied the second floor of a South Street firetrap, above a tonsorial parlor and a washhouse. You might have missed it if you weren't on the lookout, for the only sign was wired to a support post at the foot of an outside staircase. The sign was some two feet square with faded lettering and a painted arrow pointing upward; a reversible card in a metal holder stated that the club was open.

Quincannon climbed the stairs alone, there being no need for Flannery's presence here. The door at the top opened into a long, wide room bisected lengthwise by a waist-high partition, the room's plain furnishings and lack of adornments indicating that its clientele was primarily farmhands, fishermen, and other members of the working class. One side was taken up with half a dozen round poker tables covered with green baize, all of which were deserted. On the other side were several smaller tables for those who preferred different card games; two elderly men, the only customers at this early hour, sat at one playing a desultory game of pinochle. At the rear was a short buffet, above which was tacked a placard that read: **Beer 10c. No Hard Liquor.**

Just inside the entrance stood a kind of three-sided cage presided over by a heavy-set man wearing a green eyeshade and thick galluses over a green and white striped shirt. Strangers in the Ace High were evidently a rarity; he looked Quincannon up and down, taking his measure.

"If poker's your game, friend," he said, "you've come too early, as you can see. Likely won't be a game of stud or draw until this afternoon."

Quincannon showed him an amiable smile. "It's a man I'm looking for, not a poker game."

"What man would that be?"

"The assayer, Bart Morgan. I was told he is a regular here when he's in town."

"Told by who?"

"Floyd Tucker, his assistant."

"If you saw Tucker, then he must've also told you his boss hasn't been around for two weeks or more."

"He did, but it's important that I talk to Mr. Morgan as soon as possible. Would you be Luke Jaeger?"

"I would."

"Well, Tucker said you might be able to tell me where Morgan resides."

"What makes him think I'd know?"

"Just that you and Morgan might be friends, seeing as how you both fancy five-card stud."

Jaeger tugged at one of his galluses. "What's so important that you need to talk to him? Assay business?"

"Mining business, yes."

"You don't look like a prospector."

"I'm not. Engineer." The two pinochle players had their ears cocked, listening to the conversation; Quincannon lowered his voice. "I made a discovery Morgan is sure to be interested in, once he verifies its potential."

"Rich discovery? Why go to him with it?"

"I have my reasons. *Do* you know where he lives?"

"Suppose I do," Jaeger said. "Why should I help feather his nest?"

"And why not, if you're a friend of his?"

"I wouldn't call him a friend. He took close to a hundred dollars off me the last stud game at his house."

"So you've been to his house. Located where?"

"What's in it for me if I tell you?"

"Morgan's undying gratitude. And mine."

"Hah. Man can't eat or drink gratitude."

Quincannon put a hitch on his impatience, another on his distaste for parting with hard-earned money even in a good cause. He said, "A man can do both with a five-dollar gold piece."

"Let's see the color of it."

Quincannon pinched out one of two Liberty coins in his purse, held it up, then drew it quickly back when Jaeger reached for it. "An honest answer first, Mr. Jaeger."

"I always give honest answers when I'm paid for them. All right. Bart's place is over in Sacramento, on F Street."

"Where on F Street?"

"I don't recall the number. Off Fourteenth, not far from Washington Park. Red brick house with a crabapple tree in front."

"He lives there alone, does he?"

"With his wife. I'd watch out for her if I were you."

"Why is that?"

"Likes brandy, Mrs. Morgan does. Got a mean tongue when she likes too much of it, which is most of the time."

"I'll remember that."

"No charge for the advice," Jaeger said, and stretched out his hand, palm up. Quincannon dropped the coin into it, not without reluctance.

Morgan's home was in midtown Sacramento, in a residential neighborhood Flannery identified as Boulevard Park. There was a certain irony in the fact that only a few dozen blocks separated it from the Golden Eagle Hotel. If only some knowledge of its whereabouts had been available yesterday! But Flannery swore that he'd checked the residential listings and property ownership records and there had been none for B. or Bartholomew Morgan. Shrewd cuss that Morgan was, he must have seen to it that the house was put in his wife's name, married or maiden, or another of his aliases.

On F Street near 14th, red brick, crabapple tree in front . . . It was easy enough to find. Quincannon gave it a quick study as Flannery drove past on the cobblestone street. Fairly large and well landscaped, testimony to the profits Morgan had obtained through his various criminal ventures. The front windows were draped and there was no activity outside. A driveway led along one side to a carriage barn at the rear.

Near the end of the block Quincannon said to Flannery, "Drive around the corner. Let's see if there is a carriageway behind Morgan's house."

There was, a narrow lane that bisected the block straight through to the next street. "Stop here and let me out," he said then. "I'll walk back. You drive on in and keep watch at the rear."

Sabina said as Flannery braked at the entrance to the carriageway, "You can't just walk up bold as you please and knock on the door, John. Suppose Morgan sees and recognizes you before you can get the drop on him."

"I had no direct dealings with him in Patch Creek," Quincannon said. "He may have noticed me among the miners, but he wouldn't recognize me in these clothes."

"He might if he spied you coming alone. He'd be much less likely to pay attention to the approach of a man and a woman."

He had to admit that she had a point. But he said, "No. Too dangerous."

"Stop treating me as if I were fragile goods. I'm perfectly capable of taking care of myself and you know it." She patted her reticule. "I'm armed, don't forget."

He wasn't likely to. She seldom ventured out on serious business without her Remington derringer, a twin of his.

Before he could say anything more, she opened the door on her side and stepped down. He swung down beside her.

"Well, John?"

There was nothing to be gained in arguing with a headstrong woman; it would only waste time. Besides, she *was* perfectly capable of taking care of herself. "All right. Just let me do the talking."

She slipped her hand inside the crook of his left arm while he made sure his coat flap covered the holstered Peacemaker. Flannery prodded the blue dun into the carriageway behind them as they set off.

There were no pedestrians on F Street, nor any street traffic after a hansom cab clattered past. The sky had partially cleared and a pale sun laid streaks of light on the cobblestones. Except for the distant barking of a dog, the neighborhood was wrapped in a somnolent hush.

Sabina said something inconsequential, smiling as they turned onto the Morgan property—a casual pretense in the event they were being observed. Quincannon watched the windows; the curtains remained still. On the porch he paused to listen, heard nothing from within. Sabina released his arm, stood aside when he drew the Peacemaker. He slid the weapon quickly inside his coat, holding it close to his chest, then twisted the crank handle on the doorbell with his left hand.

The door stayed closed, the interior silent. After half a minute he twisted the bell handle again. Another fifteen seconds crept away. Nobody home? More vexation if that was the case—

Footsteps inside.

Quincannon tensed as the latch rattled. But when the door squeaked open, it was not Morgan he faced but a harridan incongruously draped in a purple sateen dress and a lemon-yellow feather boa. Middle-aged, stout, so tightly corseted her formidable bosom bulged the dress's bodice to the ripping point. Blotchy red face, dyed black hair, squinty gray bloodshot eyes. And according to the brandy fumes emanating from her open mouth, well on her way to inebriation at a few minutes past noon.

The squinty eyes shifted from him to Sabina and back to him. In a surprisingly clear voice she said, "Who're you? What do you want?"

"Are you Mrs. Morgan?"

"What if I am? Don't tell me you're missionaries looking to convert me. I'll spit in your eye if you are."

"We're not missionaries. Is your husband here?"

"What d'you want with him?"

"An important business matter. Is he here?"

"No. Business, you say? What kind?"

"The kind he specializes in. And I don't mean assaying."

"He know you and this business of yours?"

"Yes."

"Profitable?"

"Very. For all concerned."

That put a smile on her blotchy face. "What's your name?"

". . . Frinke. Horatio Frinke."

The squinty eyes shifted to Sabina again. "Who's she?"

"My wife."

"Pretty." Then, with a kind of drunken wistfulness, "I was pretty myself once, long time ago."

Quincannon didn't believe it, but Sabina lied tactfully, "You're still a handsome woman, Mrs. Morgan."

"Hah. I like you, missus—you lie like a politician. You in on this deal with your man and mine?"

"Yes."

"Mr. Morgan never lets me in on his deals. But that's all right, long as he brings home the bacon."

"You expect him back soon?" Quincannon asked.

"Not today. Not for a few days."

Hell and damn! "Where did he go?"

"San Francisco."

"To see whom?"

"Tell you if I knew, but I don't."

"Does he travel there often?"

"When he has reason, good reason."

"When did he leave?"

"Last night while I was asleep, like always." She leaned against the doorjamb, her thick lips twisting into a grin like a rictus. "Went to say goodbye to his lady friend."

"Lady friend?"

"Don't know this one's name. Don't care, long as he don't stop bringing home the bacon."

"Did he go by train?"

"Not to see her, he didn't."

"To San Francisco. By train or by steamer?"

"Always takes the train. Four o'clock."

"Four a.m., you mean?"

"Hah. Him get out of a chippy's bed that early? No."

"Four this afternoon, then."

"I just said so, didn't I. What time is it now?"

"Shortly past noon."

"So you're in luck. Plenty of time to catch him at the depot."

Quincannon's smile was wolfish. "We'll try to do just that."

"Tell him I said I'll be waiting for the bacon." And with that she pushed away from the jamb and banged the door shut.

On the sidewalk Sabina said with a raised eyebrow and a rib-nudge, "Horatio Frinke?"

"It was the only name I could think of on the spur."

"I must say I'm glad it's not your real name. I wouldn't fancy being Mrs. Horatio Frinke."

They hurried to the corner, around it into the carriageway. Sabina said then, "Delightful woman, Mrs. Morgan. Why do you suppose he's stayed with her all these years? She must be a devil to live with."

Quincannon grunted. His mind was on Morgan's planned trip to San Francisco. Was that where he sold the stolen gold? Or did he have some other reason for going there?

Sabina was still pondering. "It can't be because she permits him to have lady friends. Perhaps he still loves her."

"More likely he's afraid she'll expose him for the crook he is," Quincannon said as they reached the waiting brougham, "unless he keeps bringing home the bacon."

24

SABINA

In the carriage John repeated what Mrs. Morgan had told them. Flannery said, "Four o'clock. If she was right about the time, it'll be the Espee's Capitol Express that he's taking. That presents a potential problem, if you're thinking of putting the arm on him before he boards."

"Just what I was thinking. Why a potential problem?"

"The four o'clock Express is usually crowded. There'll be quite a few passengers getting off, in addition to those waiting to board. He might slip past us. Or start a ruckus if we do try to brace him."

Sabina said, "And we don't want to risk the chance of harm to innocent bystanders."

"The one other option," John said, "I like even less."

"Allow him to board and take passage ourselves."

"Yes. Watch for an opportunity to yaffle him on the train, and if none presents itself, then look to make the pinch in Oakland."

"Same potential problems in both cases," Flannery said.

John nodded agreement. "The sooner he's in custody the better. We'll have to take him at the depot here if it can be managed."

"Is there enough time to bring in the authorities?" Sabina asked. "Or men in your employ, Mr. Flannery?"

"I doubt it."

"Too many explanations required at any rate," John said. "As it is, we'll have just enough time to make preparations for both contingencies."

They drove to the Golden Eagle Hotel, made short work of packing their luggage and checking out, and then proceeded to a gunsmith Flannery knew on M Street, where John purchased a Webley five-shot pocket revolver. He did not want to go up against Morgan with his derringer, a wise decision. Flannery offered to sell him the Colt Peacemaker, but the price he quoted earned John's scorn. Besides, he said, whereas the derringer was too small, the Peacemaker was too large and cumbersome, and he would have no use for it in San Francisco.

The main depot served a number of rail lines, Flannery told them, the primary ones for the transport of intrastate passengers being the Southern Pacific—or Espee, as Flannery had called it—and the Central Pacific; the Union Pacific provided weekly transcontinental service between Oakland and Council Bluffs, Iowa, but its crack streamliner, the Golden Gate Special, was not due this day. Neither was the Golden State Limited, the Espee's transcontinental flyer.

The station was as crowded as Flannery had said it would be, with a constant stream of people embarking and disembarking on trains headed in all directions. The parking areas, waiting rooms, and platforms were teeming when they arrived shortly past three. As early as it was, John did not expect Bart Morgan to have arrived yet, but he and Flannery roamed through the throng to make sure.

Sabina, meanwhile, entrusted her carpetbag and John's war bag to one of the porters, whom she tipped generously to keep a watchful eye on them. She then approached the station agent and used her feminine charm to find out whether or not B. or Bart or Bartholomew Morgan had booked a private compartment on the Capitol Express. He hadn't. There was only one first-class Pullman and all but one of the compartments had been reserved for couples, the lone exception being a local physician known to the agent. Morgan's passage, then, was to be by day coach.

Coach tickets were still available; Sabina bought two. After which she herself searched for some sign of their quarry among the milling throng, with no better results than John and Flannery were having. She returned to wait with the porter and their luggage at the rendezvous point.

Three-thirty came and went, uneventfully.

So did three forty-five.

And three fifty-five.

The westbound Capitol Express lumbered into the station at three fifty-seven, only twelve minutes behind its scheduled arrival. The crowds were even thicker now, the platform clogged with men, women, children disembarking, about to board, or present to greet or say goodbye to friends and family members, and uniformed porters trundling baggage carts. Morgan must have put in an appearance by this time, but Sabina saw no sign of him, or of John and Flannery.

Four oh-five.

The last of the arriving passengers detrained and those departing began to board. Two more minutes passed. Where was John? He—

There he was, pushing his way toward her through the crowd. He came running up, his jaw set tight, his eyes sparking with anger and vexation. "Blasted devil slipped past us and was already in the boarding line when I spied him. Too late then to risk taking him."

"Which day coach is he in?"

"Second of the three."

"Did he see you, recognize you?"

"If he did he gave no indication of it."

"We'll have to travel with him, then."

"No other choice, confound it."

They still had enough time, barely, for the whistle hadn't sounded yet. Sabina issued swift instructions to the porter, pressed a coin into his hand to speed him on his way to the baggage car with their luggage. Then she and John ran for the second coach, reaching it just before the whistle blew and the conductor gave forth with his "All aboard!" cry. John boosted her into the vestibule, clambered up beside her. Out on the station platform she saw Flannery appear and wave: he had seen them board.

The coach was almost completely filled, many of the seats occupied by women and children, and it took her a moment to locate Morgan. Dressed in a lightweight slack suit and derby hat, he occupied a seat at the rearward end, facing in their direction, but he seemed to take no notice of them; his eyes were on a satchel he held clutched on his lap with both hands. There were two empty rearward-facing seats at the forward end, not adjacent, but John soon remedied that by politely asking a plump woman next to one of the empties if she minded moving so he could sit next to his wife who was with child. The woman nodded smiling assent and promptly moved.

Sabina leaned close to him when they were seated and whispered, "Wife with child. Really, John."

"Had the desired effect, did it not."

Steam hissed as the locomotive's brakes were released, couplings banged, and the Capitol Express jerked into motion. The time, by the tiny gold watch pinned to the bosom of Sabina's shirtwaist, was four-fifteen. Morgan still sat with his gaze cast downward at his lap.

"You don't suppose the gold is in that satchel?" Sabina murmured.

"Possibly. But he'd be a fool to carry valuables in there. Purse snatchers abound in train station crowds."

"In his checked luggage, then?"

"Not much safer. If he has it with him, likely it's in a money belt."

The train rattled through the yards. It was noisy in the coach, some of the youngsters indulging in rambunctious behavior. Stuffy, too, the air thickened by food odors and human effluvium. Sabina wished again, as she had on the trip to Sacramento, that this was one of the Espee's luxury trains such as the Golden State Limited on the San Francisco–Chicago run.

The Golden State was ventilated by a new process which renewed the air inside several times every hour, instead of having it circulated only slightly by sluggish fans. It was also said to be brightly lighted by electricity generated from the axles of the moving cars, rather than being murkily lit by oil lamps, though the dim light was advantageous under the present circumstances.

"What are you going to do, John?"

"I don't know yet."

"You can't brace him in here."

"No. I don't dare draw my weapon—it might cause a panic. And he's bound to be armed. I wouldn't put it past him to fire his pistol if he were able. Or to take a hostage."

The conductor appeared, collecting tickets. He was a spare, sallow-faced man who wore his uniform and cap as if they were badges of honor. The brass buttons shone, as did a heavy gold watch chain and its polished elk's tooth fob. A shiny badge on the front of his uniform identified him as Mr. Bridges.

Sabina dipped her chin in his direction. "Take the conductor into your confidence?"

"Not that, either," John said. "There is nothing he could do until after Morgan is in my custody, and little enough then. No, there's only one viable option, and that problematical—follow him if he leaves his seat and hope to catch him alone between cars."

"Still a high-risk proposition."

"Not necessarily. Don't worry, I won't make any move that endangers others."

The Capitol Express picked up speed, soon crossed the

railroad bridge spanning the river. Morgan hadn't moved except to lift and turn his head toward the window at his side; he seemed oblivious to everyone else in the coach. John sat statue-still, covertly watching him. Sabina shifted position on the thin seat cushion, seeking comfort and thinking that if she'd known for certain that they would be taking the train, she would have changed into her more suitable traveling clothes before leaving the hotel.

They were entering open country now, marshy in places near the river, mostly cattle graze and farmland stretching beyond. The steady, throbbing rhythm of steel on steel had a welcome muting effect on the youngsters' piping voices. A strand of Sabina's hair had come loose from its coil; she was in the process of repinning it when she felt John stiffen beside her. The reason, she saw then, was that Morgan was rising from his seat. He yawned, stretched, and then stepped into the aisle with the satchel still clutched in both hands. Balanced against the swaying motion of the car, he walked past where she and John were sitting without so much as an eye flick in their direction.

As soon as he passed through the connecting door to the coach behind, John was on his feet. He gestured for her to remain seated, followed after Morgan.

Sabina sat tensely, waiting.

25

QUINCANNON

Morgan went through the packed third day coach, through the first-class Pullman and the dining and lounge cars, past men's and women's lavatories into the smoking car. Quincannon had no chance to brace him along the way, for Morgan moved at a smart pace and there were other people in the aisles in all four cars.

Quincannon paused outside the smoking car door; through the glass he watched his quarry sit down at the far end, facing back toward the entrance, then produce a cigar from his coat pocket, fit it into the amber holder, and snip off the end with a pair of gold cutters. Settling in there, evidently, as he'd settled into the day coach. Blast the man and blast the luck!

He debated the advisability of entering, decided to take the chance. Morgan paid no attention to him when he claimed a seat just inside the door. The car was three-quarters full, smoke from cigars, pipes, cigarettes creating a thickly swirling haze.

Quincannon tugged his briar and tobacco pouch from an inside coat pocket, opened the pouch—and then stayed his hand as he was about to dip the pipe bowl inside.

Morgan was on his feet again. His cigar unlit, an expression of mild distress on his lean features, he came striding forward with eyes front as he passed where Quincannon sat. What was this? Ah, the sudden call of nature, evidently, for he stopped at the door to the men's lavatory, found it unoccupied, and closed himself inside.

Quincannon's mouth pinched into a tight smile. This might well be the break he'd been waiting for. He stowed his pipe and pouch, stood, and took up a position near the lavatory door as if waiting his turn to enter. If no one was in the immediate vicinity when Morgan emerged, he would crowd the man back inside and use his superior size and strength in that small space to subdue and disarm him—club him into unconsciousness if such proved necessary.

Waiting, watching the lavatory door, he gripped the handle of the Webley revolver in his coat pocket. A hefty individual in the flashy dress of a traveling drummer came in from the lounge, staggering slightly when couplings clashed and the car lurched as its wheels passed over a rough section of track. Outside the windows, a series of low hills, shadowed by the waning afternoon light, created a barren backdrop for a patchwork of plowed and unplowed fields.

The door to the lavatory remained closed.

A prickly sensation formed between Quincannon's shoulder blades. How long had Morgan been in there? It had to be more than five minutes now. One of the other occupants left the smoking car; a fat man, his round face adorned with a thicket of muttonchop whiskers, came in. The fat gent paused, glancing around, then turned to the lavatory door and tried the latch. When he found it locked, he rapped on the panel. There was no response.

The prickly sensation grew as hot as a fire-rash. Quincannon prodded the fat man aside, ignoring the indignant oath this brought him, and laid an ear against the panel. All he could hear were train sounds: the pound of beating trucks on the fishplates, the creek and groan of axle play, the whisper of the wheels. He hammered on the panel with his fist, much harder than the fat fellow had. Once, twice, three times. This likewise produced no response.

"Hell and damn!"

The ejaculation brought him the attention of the remaining smokers, and so startled the fat man that he did a quick about-face and went through the connecting door onto the iron-plated vestibule, where he nearly collided with another man just stepping through. The newcomer was the conductor, Bridges, who had evidently heard the hammering and outcry while passing through the lounge car.

"Here, now, what's all the commotion?"

Quincannon snapped, "A man went into the lavatory some time ago, hasn't come out. And hasn't made a sound."

"Well, perhaps he isn't feeling well—"

"Use your master key and we'll soon know."

"I can't do that, sir, on your word alone—"

Quincannon took hold of the conductor's coat sleeve, drew him back into the vestibule out of earshot. He said, low and sharp, "I am a San Francisco detective—Quincannon, John Frederick Quincannon. The man who went into the lavatory is a dangerous fugitive. The only reason I haven't taken him into custody is concern for the safety of the other passengers."

The fervency of Quincannon's words and demeanor brooked no argument, and brought none. "Good Lord!" the conductor said in shocked tones. "What did he do? Who is he?"

"I'll explain later; there's no time now."

"You don't think he—"

"Open the door, Mr. Bridges, and be quick about it."

The conductor unlocked the lavatory door. Quincannon pushed in first, his hand on the butt of the Webley revolver—and immediately blistered the air with a five-jointed oath.

The cubicle was empty.

"By all the saints!" Bridges said behind him. "He must have gone through the window and jumped."

The lone window was small, designed for ventilation, but not too small for a man Morgan's size to wiggle through. Quincannon, if he'd tried it, would have gotten stuck halfway through. It was shut but not latched; he hoisted the sash, poked his head out. The stinging slipstream made him pull it back in again. A futile effort at any rate, for there had been nothing worth seeing.

"Gone, yes," he said, "but I'll eat my hat if he jumped at the rate of speed we've been traveling."

"But . . . he must have. The only other place he could have gone . . ."

"Up atop the car. That's where he did go."

The conductor didn't want to believe it. His thinking was plain: if the dangerous fugitive Quincannon was after had leaped out, he was rid of a threat to his passengers' security. He said, "A climb like that can be almost as lethal as jumping."

"Not for an agile and desperate man."

"He couldn't hide up there. Nor for long on top of any of the cars. There is nowhere for him to hide inside, either—the only possible places are too easily searched. He must know that if he's familiar with trains."

Quincannon had nothing to say to that.

Bridges asked, "Do you think he crawled along the roofs, then climbed back down between two other cars?"

"It's the likeliest explanation."

"Why would he do such a thing?"

Why? The answer was obvious enough to Quincannon, bitterly so. Morgan must have recognized him on the platform or in the coach, from a description furnished by Walrus Ben, and confirmed the recognition when he was followed into the smoking car. He also must have guessed that J. F. Quinn was a detective employed to investigate the high-grading—the primary reason he'd left Patch Creek so abruptly on Sunday. For all Morgan knew now there were other lawmen on board or waiting at the Capitol Express's first stop in Vacaville; he couldn't take the chance of waiting to find out, not with the stolen gold dust in his possession, as it surely was in a belt buckled around his middle. If there had been anything of value in the satchel, he had removed whatever it was before chucking the bag through the window and climbing out.

The actions of a desperate man, but also a cunning one. Morgan had some sort of escape plan in mind, or else he would not have taken the risk he had.

Bridges asked anxiously, "Who is he? What crimes did he commit?"

"His name is Morgan, Bartholomew Morgan. A thief, among other criminal offenses."

"You said he's dangerous. Do you think he's armed?"

"No question of it."

"Oh, Lordy. What does he look like?"

Quincannon provided a cogent description. "The birthmark should make him easy enough to spot. If he tries to conceal it under a stolen garment, that will give him away too."

"So you think he'll attempt to blend in with the other passengers?"

"Unless he has another trick up his sleeve. How long to the Vacaville stop?"

Bridges checked his railroad watch. "Forty minutes."

"That should give us plenty of time for a search. Every nook and cranny from locomotive to caboose, if necessary."

"If we don't find him, what then?"

"We'll find him," Quincannon said darkly. "He is still on this train, Mr. Bridges. He can't have gotten off."

While Bridges stood watch, Quincannon stepped through the vestibule doorway and carefully climbed to the top of the iron ladder outside. He peered over the roofs of the cars, protecting his eyes with an upraised arm, for the coal-flavored smoke that rolled back from the locomotive's stack was peppered with hot cinders. As expected, he saw no sign of his quarry. But he did find evidence of the man's passage: marks in the thin grit that coated the tops of the lounge car as well as the smoking car, indicating that Morgan had gone forward.

Back in the vestibule, he used his handkerchief to cleanse his hands and face. The grimy streaks on the cloth confirmed another fact: no matter how long Morgan had been above or how far he'd crawled, his clothing had to be soiled when he came down. Someone may have seen him. And he couldn't have wandered far in that condition. Either he was hiding where he lighted—one of the Pullman compartments, mayhap—or he would take the time to wash up and brush his clothes.

Quincannon said as much to the conductor, who responded, "I still say it makes no sense. Not a lick of sense."

"It does to him. And it will to us when we find him."

They worked their way forward, making sure Morgan wasn't closeted in any of the lavatories, Bridges quietly alerting members of the crew. Their inspection of the lounge and dining cars was cursory. Morgan, shrewd as he was, could not have hoped to pass undetected in either one and so had avoided them.

When they reached the first-class Pullman, Bridges began knocking on compartment doors. No one in those occupied had seen Morgan. Nor was he in either of two temporarily empty compartments; Bridges' passkey allowed searches of both. By the time they finished, the urgency and frustration both men felt were taking a toll: Quincannon nearly bowled over a pudgy matron outside the first-class women's lavatory, and Bridges snapped at a pompous gent who demanded to know what the devil was going on.

It took them five minutes to scan through the passengers in the third day coach—another exercise in futility. When they entered the middle coach, Sabina rose as soon as she saw them. Quincannon beckoned her out onto the vestibule, where he introduced her to Bridges—"My partner, Mrs. Sabina Carpenter"—and gave her a terse account of the situation. She received the news stoically; unlike him, she met most crises with a shield of calm.

She said, "He's not in the second coach. I would have noticed any newcomers, especially one with the side of his face covered."

"Almost certainly not in the first then, either. He wouldn't have crawled that far over the tops of the cars."

No, Morgan was not in the first coach. A swift search proved that.

In the vestibule again, Sabina said, "The man may be full of tricks, but he can't make himself invisible. He has to be somewhere."

"Not the tender or the locomotive," Bridges said. "There's no way he could get into either one without being seen and thwarted."

"Which leaves the baggage car and the caboose."

"He couldn't get into those, either."

Quincannon said, "Are you sure about the baggage car?"

"The baggage master secures all the doors as soon as we depart."

He bit back a self-deprecating expletive in deference to Sabina. "Blast it, we should have checked there before we came forward. But it's not too late if we hurry, Mr. Bridges."

Sabina said, "I'll go with you—"

"No need. Take a slow stroll through the cars on the off chance we somehow overlooked him among the passengers."

She didn't argue.

The baggage master's office was empty. Beyond, the door to the baggage car stood open a few inches.

Frowning, Bridges stepped up to the office door, tried the latch. Unlocked. "Oh, Lordy," he said in a choked whisper, then opened the door and called out, "Dan? You in the car?"

No answer.

The hot prickly sensation was back between Quincannon's shoulder blades. He drew the Webley, shouldered the conductor aside, and crossed the office to widen the doorway to the baggage car. The oil lamps inside were lighted; most of the interior was visible. Boxes, crates, stacks of luggage and express parcels, but no sign of human habitation.

"What do you see, Mr. Quincannon?"

"Nothing. No one."

"I don't like this, none of this," Bridges said. "Where's Dan? He's always here, and he never leaves doors unlocked . . ."

Quincannon eased his body through the doorway and into a crouch behind a packing crate. Peering out, he saw no one and no evidence of disturbance anywhere. Several large crates and trunks were belted in place along the inner wall. Against the far wall stood a pair of carts piled with luggage. More of the same rested in neat rows nearby, among them Sabina's carpetbag and his war bag. None of the baggage appeared to have been tampered with, or moved except by the natural motion of the train.

Toward the front was a shadowed area into which he could not see clearly. A possible hiding place? He straightened, edged around and alongside the crate with the revolver cocked and ready. No sounds other than the thrum of steel on steel. And no movement until a brief lurch and shudder as the locomotive nosed into a curve and the engineer used his air. Then something slid into view in the dusky corner.

A leg. A man's leg, twisted and bent.

Quincannon muttered the expletive he had suppressed earlier, closed the gap by another half dozen paces. He could see the rest of the man's body then—a sixtyish fellow in a trainman's uniform, lying crumpled, his cap off and a dark blotch staining his wispy gray hair. Quincannon went to one knee beside him, found a thin wrist, and pressed it for a pulse. The beat was there, faint and irregular.

"Mr. Bridges! Be quick!"

The conductor came running inside. When he saw the unconscious crewman he jerked to a halt; a moaning sound vibrated in his throat. "My God, old Dan! Is he—?"

"No. Wounded but still alive."

"Shot?"

"Struck with something hard. A gun butt, like as not."

"Morgan, damn his eyes."

"He was after something in here," Quincannon said. "We'll take a quick look around. Tell me if you notice anything missing or out of place."

"What about Dan? One of the drawing-room passengers is a doctor . . ."

"Fetch him. But look around first."

They took a turn through the car. None of the belted boxes and crates showed signs of having been tampered with, nor did any of the hand luggage. If Morgan had gotten into any of the baggage, he had done a good job of covering up afterward. But why would he have bothered?

Bridges confirmed that as far as he could tell, nothing was amiss. "But Dan is the only one who'll know for sure."

"One thing before you go. Are you carrying weapons of any kind? Rifles, handguns in unmarked boxes? Or dynamite or black powder?"

"None by manifest or declaration, thank heaven."

Bridges hurried away. Quincannon pillowed the baggage master's head on one of the smaller bags, noting that the blood on and around his wound had begun to coagulate. The assault must have taken place not long after Morgan's disappearance from the lavatory. The foxy devil had anticipated a check of the tops of the cars, marked the grit on the lounge car to give the false impression that he'd gone forward, then crawled back here. Damnation! If they had thought to check the baggage car first thing, they might have caught him in the act.

But this was no time for recriminations. Whatever Morgan's reason for coming here, it had to be an integral part of the escape plan he'd devised. Yes, but he still had no idea what that could possibly be.

26

QUINCANNON

The doctor was young, brusque, and efficient. Quincannon and Bridges left old Dan in his care, hurried forward again.

As they passed through the dining car, the locomotive's whistle sounded a series of short toots.

"Oh, Lordy," the conductor said. "That's the first signal for Vacaville."

"How long before we arrive at the depot?"

"Ten minutes."

"Blast!"

They came upon Sabina in the Pullman car; she shook her head.

Quincannon was beside himself by this time. The entire rolling stock had been carefully searched now, front to back. So where the bloody hell was Morgan?

They held a huddled conference. Quincannon's latest piece of bad news ridged the smoothness of Sabina's forehead, her only outward reaction. "You're certain nothing was taken from the baggage car?" she asked Bridges.

"As certain as I can be without a thorough examination and the cooperation of the passengers."

"If Morgan did steal something," Quincannon said, "he was careful not to call attention to the fact, in case the baggage master regained consciousness before he could make good his escape."

"Which could mean," Sabina said, "that whatever it was would have been apparent to us at a cursory search."

"Either that, or where it was taken from would have been apparent."

Something seemed to be nibbling at her mind; her expression turned speculative. "I wonder . . ."

"What do you wonder?"

The locomotive's whistle sounded again. There was a rocking motion and the loud thump of couplings as the engineer began the first slackening of their speed. Bridges said, "Five minutes to the Vacaville station. If Morgan is still on board—"

"He is."

"—do you think he'll try to get off there?"

"No doubt of it. Wherever he's hiding, he can't hope to avoid being discovered in a concentrated search. And he knows we'll mount one in Vacaville with the train crew and the local authorities."

"What do you advise we do?"

"Assign someone to summon the law as soon as we arrive at the station," Quincannon said. "Then tell your porters not to allow anyone off the train until you give the signal. And when passengers do disembark, they're to do so in single file from between two cars only. That will prevent Morgan from slipping off in a crowd."

"The second and third day coaches?"

"Good. Meet me in the vestibule there."

Bridges hurried off.

Quincannon said to Sabina, "You may as well take your seat until we reach the station."

"No, I have something else to do."

"Yes? What?"

"I noticed something earlier that I thought must be a coincidence. Now I'm not so sure it is."

"Explain that."

"There's no time now. You'll be the first to know if I'm right."

"Sabina . . ."

But she had already turned her back and was purposefully heading aft.

He took himself out onto the vestibule between the second and third coaches. The train had slowed to half speed; once more the whistle cut shrilly through the late afternoon stillness. He stood holding on to the hand bar and leaning out on the side away from the station to look both directions along the cars—a precaution in the event Morgan attempted to jump and run through the yards. But he was thinking that this was another exercise in futility. Morgan's scheme was surely too clever for such a predictable ending.

Bridges reappeared and stood watch on the offside as the train entered the rail yards. On Quincannon's side the dun-colored depot building swam into view through the fading daylight ahead. Once a pioneer settlement and Pony Express stop, Vacaville was now a thriving agricultural center widely known as the fresh fruit capital of California. But it was nonetheless a small town, so relatively few passengers would be waiting to board. Even if Morgan managed to get off the train here, he couldn't reasonably expect to escape detection and capture. Yet it was utter folly for him to remain hidden on the Capitol Express.

He *had* to be planning to exit here, but how? A diversion of some sort? That was the most probable gambit. Quincannon warned himself to be alert for anything at all out of the ordinary.

Sabina was on his mind, too. Where had she gone in such a hurry? What sort of coincidence . . . ?

Brake shoes squealed on the rails as the Express neared the lighted station platform. He'd been right in his estimate of the number of those waiting; less than a score of men and women stood beneath a roof overhang. He swiveled his head again. Steam and smoke clouded the gathering dusk, but he could see clearly enough. No one was making an effort to leave the train on this side. Nor on the offside, or else Bridges would have cut loose with a shout.

The engineer brought the cars to a rattling stop alongside the platform. Quincannon dropped off, with Bridges close behind him. At the same time a porter jumped down from between the two forward cars, raced off through a cloud of steam on his mission to fetch the local law.

Minutes passed. Quincannon's eyes moved restlessly back and forth along the length of the rolling stock. Through the windows he could see passengers lining up for departure; Sabina, he was relieved to note, was one of them, in the forefront. Another porter stood in the vestibule between the second and third coaches, waiting for the signal from Bridges to put down the steps.

Some of the embarking passengers began voicing complaints at the delay, and Bridges took command of the situation. What he said by way of explanation Quincannon didn't hear, but it succeeded in quieting them. With the aid of the station agent, he herded them all off the platform and into the safety of the depot.

It was another five tense minutes before the law arrived, in the person of the police chief and two deputies. The chief, who gave his name as Hoover, was burly and sported a large drooping mustache; on the lapel of his frock coat he wore a five-pointed star, and holstered at his belt was a heavy Colt Dragoon.

He said to Bridges, "You have a fugitive on board your train, is that right?"

"Yes."

"Who is he? What's he done?"

"Ask Mr. Quincannon here. He's a detective from San Francisco on the man's trail."

"That so? Police detective?"

Quincannon said, "Private. Carpenter and Quincannon, Professional Detective Services."

"Oh, a flycop." Hoover was not impressed, but neither did he show any hostility. A man not given to rushes in judgment. "Well? What's this all about?"

Quincannon explained in concise terms, stating for emphasis that Morgan was the man responsible for a series of gold robberies and likely in possession of some of the loot.

Now Hoover was impressed. "You say you searched everywhere, every possible hiding place," he said. "If that's so, how can this thief Morgan still be on the train?"

"That question has no answer yet. But he is—I'll stake my reputation on it."

"Well, then, we'll find him." The police chief turned to Bridges. "Conductor, disembark your passengers. All of 'em, not just those for Vacaville."

"Just as you say."

Bridges signaled to the porter, who swung the steps down and permitted the exodus to begin. One of the first passengers to alight was Sabina. She came straight to where Quincannon stood, took hold of his arm. Her manner was urgent, her eyes bright.

"John," she said, an edge in her voice, "I found Morgan."

Hoover said, "What's that? Who're you, madam?"

"Sabina Carpenter. Carpenter and Quincannon, Professional Detective Services."

"A *lady* flycop. Now if that don't beat all."

Quincannon had long ago ceased to be surprised at anything Sabina said or did. He asked her, "Where? How?"

She shook her head. "He'll be getting off any second."

"Getting off? With the other passengers?"

"Yes, he— There he is!"

Quincannon squinted at the passengers who were just then disembarking—two women, one of whom had a small boy in tow. "Where? I don't see him . . ."

Sabina was moving again. Quincannon trailed after her, his hand on the Webley. The two women and the child were making their way past Chief Hoover and his deputies, not paying the law any heed. The woman towing the little boy was young and pretty, with tightly curled blond hair; the other woman, older and pudgy, powdered and rouged, wore a traveling dress and a close-fitting bonnet that covered most of her head and shadowed her face. She was the one, Quincannon realized, that he had nearly bowled over outside the women's lavatory in the first-class Pullman.

She was also Bartholomew Morgan.

He found that out five seconds later, when Sabina boldly walked up and tore the bonnet off to reveal the short-haired male head and clean-shaven face hidden beneath. Her action so surprised Morgan that he had no time to do anything but swipe at her with one arm, a blow that she nimbly dodged. Then he fumbled inside the reticule he carried, pulled out the hammerless .32-caliber pistol he'd drawn at the Patch Creek poker game; in the next second he commenced a headlong flight along the platform.

Sabina shouted, Quincannon shouted, the blond woman let out a thin screech; there was a small scrambling panic among the disembarking passengers. But it lasted no more than a few seconds, and without a shot being fired.

Morgan was poorly schooled in the mechanics of running while garbed in women's clothing; the dress's long skirt tripped him before he reached the platform's end. He went down in a tangle of arms, legs, petticoats, and assorted other garments that he had wadded up and tied around his torso to create the illusion of pudginess. The fall also unveiled the other item tightly buckled around his midriff—a money belt whose pockets bulged with what was certainly the stolen gold dust.

He was still clutching the pistol when Quincannon reached him, but one well-placed kick and it went flying. Quincannon then plunged down on Morgan's chest with both knees, driving the wind out of him in a hissing grunt. Another well-placed blow, this one to the jaw, put an end to the skirmish.

Chief Hoover, his deputies, Mr. Bridges, and a gaggle of the Capitol Express's passengers stood gawping at the half-disguised and unconscious crook. Hoover was the first to speak. He murmured in awed tones, "Well, I'll be a son of a bitch."

Which mirrored Quincannon's sentiments exactly.

Morgan was soon carted off in steel bracelets to the Vacaville jail, Quincannon accompanying him, Hoover, and one deputy in the paddy wagon. Once he verified that the stolen gold dust was indeed packed into the money belt, he was not about to let it out of his sight until it was locked into the jail safe. Also put into the safe was a packet of papers that had been tucked between the belt and Morgan's belly, for they contained evidence identifying the San Francisco smelting firm that had been buying the gold. Morgan must have been carrying the packet in his satchel and later transferred it to his person.

Sabina and Bridges remained at the depot. The departure of the Capitol Express, much to the consternation of the waiting westbound passengers, was delayed a while longer. One reason was the removal of Sabina's and Quincannon's luggage from the baggage car. He'd suggested that she continue on to San Francisco, since he intended to remain in Vacaville until arrangements could be made to transport the prisoner to the Yuba County jail in Marysville where the other high-graders had been taken, and for the gold—some $13,000 worth at a rough estimate—to be returned to James O'Hearn. But she insisted on staying overnight with him here, a prospect he naturally found pleasing.

An attempt to question Morgan proved futile; he had wrapped himself in unbroken silence. This suited Quincannon well enough, but Hoover wanted to know the details of the miscreant's daring escape attempt. The situation being what it was, he had to settle for an educated guess.

Morgan had climbed out through the lavatory window, Quincannon opined, taking his satchel with him. He then crawled over the top of the smoking car and down the ladder to the baggage car, where he used some sort of ruse to get the baggage master to open up. After finding and rifling a woman passenger's suitcase, he stuffed the various items of female apparel into the satchel, mounted topside again, and crawled forward over three car roofs to the Pullman.

Once there, he waited until he was sure the first-class women's lavatory was empty, then climbed down into it through its window. He locked the door, washed and shaved off his mustache with a razor from the satchel, dressed in the stolen clothing, put on pilfered rouge and powder to cover his birthmark, and stuffed his own clothing into the satchel before dropping it through the window.

And when he left the lavatory on his way to a seat in the third day coach, Quincannon had nearly knocked him down. If only he had, he thought ruefully. It would have saved them all considerable trouble.

The one question Hoover asked that Quincannon could not satisfactorily answer was how Sabina had known Morgan was disguised as a woman. Perhaps she had gotten close enough to him while they were waiting to disembark to see through his disguise. But that didn't account for her earlier statement about coincidence or her rushing off on an unexplained errand.

He put the question to her later that evening, while they were having dinner in the Vacaville Hotel. How did she know?

"Familiarity," she said.

"Familiarity? With what?"

"Something I first thought was a coincidence but wasn't."

"So you said. Don't be enigmatic, my dear."

"I'm not, intentionally. John, you are without question a splendid detective, but there are times when you're not as observant as you might be. Tell me, what was I wearing when you met me in the lobby of the Golden Eagle Hotel last night?"

"I don't see what that has to do with—" Then, as the light dawned, he said in a smaller voice, "Oh."

"That's right," Sabina said. "The bag Morgan plundered was one of the last loaded into the baggage car. The gray serge traveling dress and Langtry bonnet he was wearing are mine."

27

SABINA

What with one thing and another, it was two weeks shy of Thanksgiving before she became Mrs. Sabina Carpenter Quincannon.

Professional matters were partly responsible. John spent two more days in Vacaville awaiting extradition orders for Bartholomew Morgan and arranging for the return of the stolen gold. Meanwhile Sabina returned to the city to find a pair of messages indicating that the agency's brief business drought had ended; one, from their best client, Great Western Insurance's claims adjuster Jackson Pollard, concerned a major fraud case she knew John would want to investigate. (He did, despite having collected his fee and a handsome bonus from a grateful Everett Hoxley, and the investigation took more than a week.) Two other, less time-consuming cases also came their way, both of which she handled herself—an absent husband who turned out to be a philanderer, and a missing set of expensive seed pearls that had been filched by a society matron's male secretary to pay off a gambling debt.

To her considerable relief, she had escaped repercussions from both of her impulse investigations. According to a brief news story in the *Morning Call,* Vernon Purifoy had been arrested and charged with embezzlement, and had accused Gretchen Kantor of stealing his private records and sending them anonymously to his employers. If Miss Kantor had any inkling that Sabina was responsible, she had been so disillusioned by her lover's betrayal that she'd chosen to remain silent. And Elmer Goodlove, whose true name the police still had not discovered, had made no statement connecting Mrs. Jonathan Fredericks with his fate.

Snags in preparations for the wedding and reception were also responsible for the delay. On the first-chosen day, Amity Wellman had a Voting Rights for Women engagement that could not be broken, necessitating a shift to the following weekend; John continued to waffle as to whom he wanted to be his best man, finally settling on his former Secret Service boss, Cecil Boggs (Cecil!), and then had some difficulty convincing Mr. Boggs to accept the honor; the minister Callie engaged to perform the service was forced to cancel on short notice due to illness in his family; Callie and the caterer had a falling-out over the reception menu which caused her to have to seek out and employ another. The only preparation that went smoothly was Sabina's search for a bridal gown. She found one that suited her in a small dressmaking shop on Geary Street: pearly white (the devil with convention), scalloped high neck, sheer lace and tiered crochet overlay, elbow-length sleeves.

The wedding, when the day finally came, took place with nary a hitch. Callie had kept her promise of restraint in furbishing her and Hugh's home for the occasion, with tasteful flower arrangements and none of her usual lavish frippery. John, handsome in formal suit and tie, was so nervous during the ceremony that he nearly dropped the wedding ring before sliding it onto her finger—a moment she found endearing. The guests, who included Jackson Pollard, Elizabeth Petrie, and another part-time agency employee, Whit Slattery, in addition to Amity and Mr. Boggs, were a convivial mix. Kamico, Amity's young Japanese ward, was exactly the right person to have caught the toss of the bridal bouquet. And the food and beverages at the reception buffet could not have been better.

The honeymoon exceeded Sabina's expectations as well. Four lovely days and nights at Boyes Hot Springs in scenic Valley of the Moon. The nights especially. So blissful were they that afterward she felt her blood quicken whenever she thought of them.

A registered package was waiting for them at the agency when they returned. Elizabeth, who had been minding the store, had signed for it and put it into the office safe. It was small, neatly wrapped, and postmarked "Salt Lake City."

"We don't know anyone in Salt Lake City," John said.

"Somebody there knows us, apparently."

Sabina removed the outer wrapping. Inside was a gift box of the sort jewelers used; inside the box was a velvet drawstring pouch and a note on a Bristol vellum card; and inside the velvet pouch . . .

Five tiny white-gold nuggets.

John peered at them gleaming in the palm of her hand. "Someone's idea of a joke," he said.

"They look genuine to me."

He picked one up, studied it, then rubbed it between his thumb and forefinger. "You're right. Real gold, by godfrey."

Sabina returned the nuggets to the velvet pouch and picked up the note.

The fine spidery hand that had penned it was familiar. Smiling, she read the message aloud. "'Felicitations, valued colleagues. My sincere apologies for the tardiness of this small gift, but I only just learned of your recent nuptials. May your union be a long and contented one.'"

"Mawkish sentiment," John said.

"Oh, I don't think so."

"Who is it from?"

"It's signed, 'With fond regards, S.H.'"

"S.H.? I know no one with those initials."

"Yes you do. Charles Percival Fairchild the Third. Better known to us as the fancied Sherlock Holmes."

"Faugh! I thought we'd heard the last of that infernal crackbrain. Five tiny white-gold nuggets . . . what kind of daft wedding present is that?"

Sabina laughed. "A *good* omen to his skewed way of thinking, considering what the nuggets are likely meant to represent."

"And that is?"

"Pips," she said. "Five orange pips."

While John was puzzling over the connection to the genuine Sherlock Holmes case, she reread the note and its two-line postscript. She hadn't quoted the postscript aloud, and would not share it with him just yet, if at all; it was liable to start him fulminating. But she had to concede that it rather pleased her.

"I shall soon return to your fair city," it read. "*Adieu, mes amis*, until we meet again."